CW00840288

I dedicate this book to i
souls of today and tomoi row, who will fight for
the wild spaces of the world.

Wilbur Smith

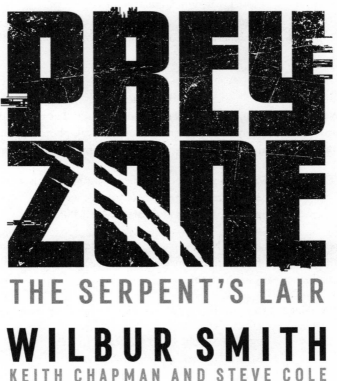

PREY ZONE

THE SERPENT'S LAIR

WILBUR SMITH

KEITH CHAPMAN AND STEVE COLE

HOT
KEY
BOOKS

First published in Great Britain in 2023 by
HOT KEY BOOKS
4th Floor, Victoria House, Bloomsbury Square
London WC1B 4DA
Owned by Bonnier Books
Sveavägen 56, Stockholm, Sweden
bonnierbooks.co.uk/HotKeyBooks

A CIP catalogue record for this book is available from the British Library.

ISBN: 978-1-4714-1295-0
Also available as an ebook and in audio

1

This book is typeset using Atomik ePublisher
Printed and bound in Great Britain by Clays Ltd, Elcograf S.p.A.

Hot Key Books is an imprint of Bonnier Books UK
bonnierbooks.co.uk

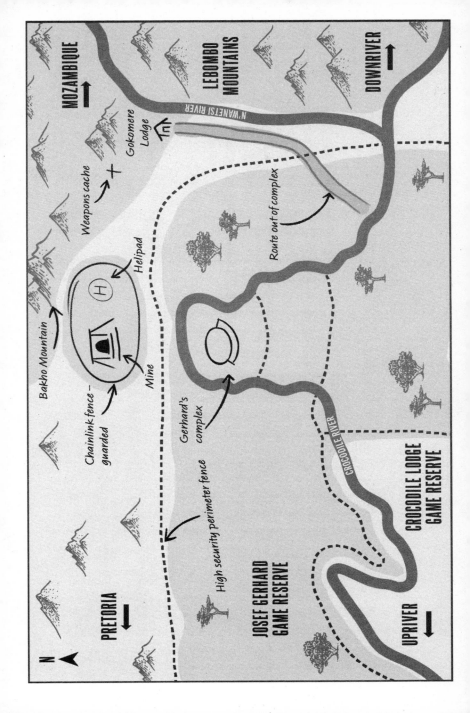

PROLOGUE

No noise-cancelling headphones in the world could drown out the sound of the woman across the aisle coughing up her lungs. Her hacking coughs were getting worse and more persistent.

Ravi sighed, turned up his music, and looked out of the aircraft window, staring out across an endless blanket of cloud. Flying business class from South Africa to the UK had been sold to him as a big treat, a kind of bribe from his mum to show that emigrating wasn't all bad, but somehow he'd landed the worst seat on the plane. Typical.

Like one fancy flight could make up for losing everything I know, anyway, Ravi thought sourly. *Just so Mum can spend all day in an office in London instead of at home in Pretoria.*

Then a message popped up on the in-flight entertainment screen in front of him.

People aren't supposed to get sick in business class! :p
Want to swap seats?

He shifted in his seat to look up the aisle. Five rows ahead, Mum was giving him a little wave. She must be feeling guilty to make the offer. But Ravi wasn't ready to let her off the hook. He shook his head and turned back to the window.

A fresh bout of wet, revolting coughing came from the woman. The attendant come over and stood beside her.

'Mrs Tate,' he said. 'May I get you another drink of water?'

'Yes, please,' the woman wheezed. 'I'm so sorry. I saw my doctor in Pretoria and he told me something new was going around . . .'

'Drink it up, Mrs Tate,' the attendant said as he handed her a bottle.

'Oh, please, do call me Rosalind.'

'When you've finished the water, may I ask you to wear this face mask?' the attendant went on smoothly. 'Is that OK? For the comfort of other passengers, you understand?'

'Yes, of course.' Mrs Tate took a few sips of the drink, then placed the mask over her mouth and nose with trembling hands. 'I'm so sorry to put you out.'

When the attendant moved aside, Ravi saw that, even with the mask covering most of her face, Rosalind Tate looked pale and clammy, with red veins threading through the whites of her eyes. She tried to smile at Ravi from behind the mask, but another coughing fit made her double over.

Ravi looked away, turned his music louder still. He'd seen some stuff online about this new mystery bug going around. *Chill*, he told himself. *Mum had Covid twice and you didn't get it.* Besides, six hours had already passed; there were only five more to go till the plane touched down in London. He saw that Mum had messaged again:

That coughing is gross! Just our luck if we catch whatever she's got!

You're such a try-hard, Mum, thought Ravi, and typed back:

I hope it's fatal.

Then he pressed send, switched off the screen and closed his eyes.

Somehow Ravi managed to fall asleep. He was only woken by the attendant telling him to fasten his seat belt for landing. Mrs Tate was still there, hunched under a fancy business class quilt, her seat belt fastened over it. She wasn't coughing any more, although she wheezed with every rapid breath.

With nothing better to do, Ravi kept an eye on her. The poor woman barely stirred through the aircraft's final descent. The landing was smooth, and once the plane was down, the attendant came straight over to Mrs Tate's seat and placed a gentle hand on her shoulder.

'Hello, Mrs Tate, we're safely down,' he said. 'Just to confirm, we've arranged a fast-track through customs so you can get on with your trip as soon as . . .'

His voice trailed away as Mrs Tate jerked in her seat as if she was having some kind of seizure. She coughed, and it sounded like her lungs were full of splinters. The attendant signalled frantically to a colleague further up the aisle for help.

Too late.

Mrs Tate's head lolled to one side. For a few seconds, she gazed at Ravi with bulging, bloodshot eyes. A crimson trickle ran from each side of her mouth.

Ravi jerked backwards in disgust. *It was just a bug*, he thought helplessly. *A stupid cough* . . .

As the cabin erupted in noisy alarm and Ravi's mum came scurrying to help her son, Rosalind Tate sat watching the scene through bloody, sightless eyes. She was quite dead.

1

Another slow and red-raw day, thought Robyn Ballantyne. The four-by-four lurched, and she was nearly sent flying from her seat for the sixth time in as many minutes. She couldn't imagine ever feeling comfortable again.

Dawn had thrown daggers of warm light through the night's shadows. As their stolen jeep climbed over higher terrain, Robyn imagined the volcanic ridges of the Lebombo Mountains past the protective shroud of the mopane trees. The vehicle moved at a crawl, nudging through the thick undergrowth, the leaves like green butterflies crowding at the windows.

Two nightmarish weeks. That was how long she'd been cooped up in this battered, overcrowded transport, moving at this painful pace through the rugged bushveld, trying to find safety. Unseasonal downpours had caused landslides all across the region, making the likeliest trails all but impassable. They had travelled by night where possible, sticking to the toughest ground in the hope their enemies would look elsewhere.

But when your enemies were a millionaire psychopath and the corrupt president of your country – with all the resources their wealth and standing could buy – could any plan stand a chance of success?

'We escaped Gerhard's compound. Got evidence of what's been going down. We've survived so much,' Robyn said to no one in particular. 'This was meant to be freedom.'

'I know,' her brother Ralph murmured beside her. 'Feels more like we're prisoners than ever.'

The time before the two of them had found the tracks of something monstrous on the banks of their home, the Crocodile Lodge Game Reserve, seemed like a different life entirely. Some impossible beast was tearing apart the proud, majestic animals Robyn loved so dearly. Looking for answers, they'd gone to the neighbouring wildlife reserve of super-rich technology developer Josef Gerhard – and there they had found more danger and horror than they could ever have imagined. For Gerhard had a high-tech lab, and there he had combined DNA from apex predators in his reserve with the DNA of prehistoric beasts to create living monsters that could have come from his video game *Predasaur*. They were the ultimate big game, and they would make the ultimate trophies for hunters rich enough to afford it. And the ultimate way for Gerhard's ally – and president of South Africa – Julius Mbato to dispose of his political opponents in the most gruesome ways imaginable.

But in bringing ancient beasts back to life, Gerhard's sick research had managed to drag something still worse into the public domain: a deadly zoonotic virus that had crossed from predasaur to human. It might already be tearing through the world's population; Robyn and Ralph had no way of knowing for sure.

After their showdown with Gerhard and Mbato two weeks ago, they'd fled into the wild, knowing they couldn't return home for fear of who would be waiting for them there. Nor could they head straight to the nearest city with their evidence – spies would be watching for them everywhere. Gerhard and Mbato were hunting down the desperate group to save themselves, so the Ballantynes and their friends were cut off from all communications and were in hiding.

They needed allies.

'Do you think we'll ever find the San who live here?' Robyn said.

'I wonder what name this community goes by,' said Ralph. 'San' was a term for the tribal people indigenous to South Africa, but some people found the word problematic, since it was often used to lump all the tribes together. Most indigenous peoples preferred to be named after the specific tribe they belonged to. But even Xai, their father's best friend and former comrade in the South African Special Forces – who was descended from local hunter gatherers – didn't know the true name of the secretive community that had once inhabited these lands.

Right now, Xai and Roland Ballantyne were leading their short convoy in a bigger truck they'd found abandoned near Gerhard's perimeter fence. They'd used it to smash through the fence, disabled all the communications and

GPS location-finding chips in the vehicle, and were now cautiously scouting the land for signs of the tribe.

'It makes sense to turn to indigenous peoples,' Robyn said, looking for reassurance. 'They'd hate a land-grabber like Gerhard on principle. And the government's treated them so badly, I'm sure they don't like Mbato either.'

'He's probably driven them all away from here,' Ralph said, and sighed. 'Well, look on the bright side. After all these adventures, we're going to be filling a hell of a lot of blank pages in the *Adventurists* book!'

Robyn nodded. Before this nightmare had begun, she and Ralph had avidly read their great-great-great-great-grandfather's memoir of his wild life at the frontiers of civilisation in the nineteenth century. Zouga Ballantyne had been called an 'adventurist' by his peers because they thought he was reckless and irresponsible, but within the family he'd become a legend of courage and resourcefulness.

'What would Zouga do now?' Robyn pondered.

'Keep fighting,' Niko Haart insisted from the driver's seat. She was Robyn's dad's partner – something Robyn still found icky, though their mum had died years ago. Niko had come to their rescue in Gerhard's park, and nearly lost her own life while saving theirs. But since they'd broken out from Gerhard's game reserve into wild country, she'd taken to repeating 'everything will be fine' over and over. Each time, it rang a little less true. 'You'll see,' she went on. 'We're going to get out of this.'

'Whatever "this" is,' Ralph said. 'Gerhard has to be

planning more than just selling the opportunity to hunt and kill his own predasaurs. He's gone to so much time, effort, expense. He'd never get back his investment.'

'We've been over this fifty times,' said Robyn wearily. 'He uses footage from the hunts to create cut-scenes for *Predasaur*. It's the biggest game franchise in the world. He's already more than rich enough, and he doesn't care. It's the achievement that matters to him, not the money. He wants to play God.'

'But in the meantime he'll play video games with the president,' Ralph scoffed. 'Well, at least Mbato's easier to read. He's using Gerhard's cash and power to help him win the next election.'

'And Gerhard will be getting something juicy in return, you can bet. Which is why the pair of them will never stop coming after us . . .' Robyn looked down at Ralph's dead mobile phone. Hidden inside it was video evidence they'd shot of Mbato hunting one of the predasaurs – linking him not only to illegally grown monsters but also to the source of the virus. It was dynamite evidence of guilt that could destroy Mbato's career – evidence that he and Gerhard would do anything to destroy.

Niko tried again. 'We have to trust your father. He's been in worse scrapes than this before. He'll bring an end to this madness.'

'At a top speed of two kilometres per day,' said Ralph, eyeing their slow progress through the jeep's window.

'You'd rather run straight into armed mercenaries or a predasaur's jaws?' Niko snapped. 'If we're spotted, Mbato will send a squad to take us out, along with the evidence, just like he did at Gauda.'

'Fair point,' said Robyn softly. The memory made her feel sick. She'd been with Niko at the small village of Gauda at the start of this whole thing, and Niko, who was a professor of epidemiology and zoonotic diseases, had been called in for her medical expertise. The people of Gauda had started to die from the mystery virus, spread by someone from Gerhard's lab, so armed mercenaries descended and destroyed the village completely – all for nothing, it turned out, since the virus had already started to spread through the wider population. It was terrifying to think how far the virus might already have spread in the outside world: it was as ravening and unstoppable as a pack of predasaurs, as relentlessly efficient at killing as a squad of mercenaries.

Robyn shuddered. With so many enemies, so many threats, how long could they stay free?

Suddenly, Niko braked hard. The jeep was going dead slow, but still Robyn and Ralph were thrown forward. A figure emerged from the foliage ahead of them, holding up a hand in greeting.

'Grant.' Robyn stared, concerned, as the teenager approached and opened her door. Warm air, floral and nutty with the scent of nearby marula blooms, brought a welcome perfume to the sweat-soaked interior of the jeep. Ralph shuffled along to make room as Grant pushed inside beside Robyn.

'Hey,' Grant said. Though he was addressing everyone, Robyn felt his eyes linger on her, and smiled.

Grant was just sixteen, six months older than Robyn, but it was as if the saying 'an old head on young shoulders' had been invented for him. His politician dad was head of the Green Freedom Party and had long campaigned against Mbato, which had led in the end to Grant being abducted and plunged into the same deadly ordeal as Robyn and her family. When they'd set off on their escape, Grant had stayed in the jeep with Robyn, Ralph and Niko, and Roland and Xai had communicated with them from the truck using encrypted short-range walkie talkies. But as the days passed and the batteries died, the kids took turns to act as messengers between the two vehicles, passing along information and instructions.

'Well, Grant?' Niko asked tensely. 'Are we any closer to finding the tribe?'

'Maybe.' Grant shrugged. 'Past the treeline there's an old dried-up riverbed that's been fed by these floods. Xai thinks it leads to a path he remembers; driving through the water would hide our tracks.'

Ralph sat up straight. 'Don't tell me our luck is finally changing?'

'Nope,' said Grant, grimacing. 'There's no easy way through the trees to get down to it. Roland's searching right now. Fingers crossed he finds a clear path.'

Ralph held up two sets of crossed fingers and looked none too subtly between Grant and Robyn. 'Is there someone else that you want? Sorry! Some*thing* else . . .'

Robyn punched his arm. 'So funny.' She'd noticed Grant giving her shy glances, as well as his share of their final ration of chocolate; she still had the very last piece tucked deep in her pocket. She spent half her time daydreaming about what things would be like if they'd met under different circumstances – and a long way away from her nosy younger brother.

Grant cleared his throat awkwardly. 'Roland asked me to tell you to wait here. If there's no way across, you'll have to reverse along this track.'

Niko said nothing, but Robyn saw how white her knuckles were, gripping the steering wheel. If anyone – or anything – was following their trail, reversing would carry them straight into danger. Robyn felt a wave of complicated sympathy. She'd resented Niko ever since she'd started dating her dad, and always used to keep her at arm's length. But now, they were all in this together, win or lose. Live or die.

'You're tired,' Robyn said. 'Why don't I take the front seat for a bit while you rest in the back here?'

Niko looked set to object, then her shoulders slumped. 'All right. Thanks. I'll take you up on that.'

Grant looked a little disappointed, but he pulled on the handle and started to open the door. 'Yeah, come on, Niko,' he said. 'You can put up with Ralph's stinky pits in the back for a –'

'*Stop!*' Ralph shouted, as the hoots and shrieks of small monkeys making their predator alarm noises echoed through the acacia trees.

Robyn jumped, and turned quickly enough to catch a flash of dusky gold. Something massive leaped at the side of their jeep. The door was thrown violently shut, knocking Grant into her. She yelled in shock as two huge paws slammed down on the window and the vehicle rocked wildly. Grant and Niko screamed as two narrowed, crimson eyes stared in at them.

'Predasaur!' Ralph shouted.

The beast was standing on its hind legs, bracing its front paws against the window. It was a cave lion, Robyn realised, almost twice the size of a regular lion. Its muzzle was scarred and half of one ear was chewed away. She had seen those scars before.

'It's the one we saw in Gerhard's reserve,' said Ralph breathlessly. 'I knew something would come after us through that hole in the fence!'

The giant lion thumped a paw against the window again, and the glass cracked. Its jaws gaped open to show fearsomely large pointed incisors.

Niko was frozen in shock. Robyn slapped her on the shoulder. 'Move!'

The jeep's engines roared into life and the vehicle lurched forward along the track. There was a rending of metal as the cave lion's heavy claws scraped against the bodywork and the creature fell away. Robyn watched it roll over and spring back to its feet, charging after them.

'It's coming!' Niko shouted, accelerating through the mopane branches, which clawed at the jeep.

'Niko, you're leaving the path!' Ralph warned her. He had grabbed the handgun from the pouch in the back of the driver's seat – they had three rounds left – but the jeep was rocking too hard for him to aim. The cave lion gave an ear-splitting roar. Through the rear windscreen, Robyn glimpsed the hefty muscles in its back legs bunch as it hurled itself towards them. The cave lion's weight gave it great momentum – and Robyn realised they could use that against it.

'Brake!' bawled Robyn. 'Now!'

Niko slammed on the brakes. The jeep jolted to a stop and the lion crashed into its roof, its hind paws thumping against the filthy rear windscreen. With a growl that was angrier still, the beast swung its huge shaggy head down and glared in at them through a side window then jumped down, drool stringing from its jaws.

'Open the window,' Ralph hissed, raising the revolver. 'Just a crack –'

A shot fired, but not from Ralph's gun. The lion fell forward. A neat, crimson bullet hole showed in the back of its head as the beast slumped to the leafy ground and lay still.

Robyn gulped in shaky breaths. 'Who shot that thing? Who's out there?'

Then they heard footsteps, and the snap of branches breaking. Something was charging towards them.

2

'Dad!' Ralph sat forward, trembling with relief, as he saw his father emerge from the greenery.

Roland Ballantyne held his rifle at the ready, his gaunt face chiselled with concern. 'Everyone all right?'

Robyn leaned over Grant and forced open the battered jeep's door. She almost pushed Grant out of the four-by-four and ran to hug her father. Ralph scrambled out after her. He shuddered as he looked down at the cave lion's body.

'Nice shot, Dad,' he said. 'But how are you here? I thought you were in the truck with Xai.'

'Just after we let Grant out and moved on, the ground gave way. The truck's rear axle's damaged. I came to get an extra jack from the back of your jeep, heard the commotion, and . . .' His words faded as they all looked at the fallen predasaur again. It had been a seriously close call.

'Thank you, sir,' Grant said solemnly.

'Good timing,' Niko agreed.

Roland gently disengaged himself from Robyn's embrace and crossed to hold Niko. Ralph looked at his sister's face as she turned away silently. Robyn was always down on Niko. She felt that Niko was trying to wipe away the memory of their mum. But Mum had died years ago of Ebola, and Ralph was glad that his dad felt able to move on now.

As he'd learned these last ten days, moving on any distance at all was definitely a good thing.

Gently pulling away from Niko, Roland crossed to the corpse of the giant lion-beast and crouched beside it. 'Incredible.' He brushed his fingers along the tufted fur of the creature's shoulders and looked up at Ralph and Robyn. 'It's more primitive than any lion I've ever seen. One of Gerhard's evolutionary throwbacks?'

'Grown in a lab,' Robyn agreed. 'I'm glad you've stopped his suffering.' She knelt beside the cave lion and placed a hand on its flank. 'Gerhard bred these animals to be in constant pain to make them wilder, more savage, a "worthy" hunt.' She shook her head. 'Poor thing. We've seen this lion before, with . . .' Her voice clogged in her throat.

'With Luke,' Ralph finished her sentence quietly.

Luke van Rok had been a family friend. His dad owned VanRok Security, which provided the video monitoring and security systems for Crocodile Lodge. With all his tech know-how, Luke had helped Ralph and Robyn get into Gerhard's reserve to investigate – but he hadn't made it back out. They'd last seen him wounded and fleeing from hyena-beasts into a gully, heard his screams as the predasaurs set upon him. Ralph shuddered at the memory.

Grant must've noticed, as he placed a comforting hand on

Ralph's shoulder. 'We'll get justice for Luke. And for Dane,' he said quietly. Dane Mellanby had been a well-known environmental activist and Grant's mentor; Ralph had seen his photo on Mbato's 'trophy board' of political opponents who had died in the sickening predasaur hunts. 'We'll get justice for everyone Mbato and Gerhard had hunted down like animals.'

'I just thought,' said Robyn. 'Gerhard hasn't been able to find us himself . . . so maybe he's sent his creations to do the job?'

'What do you mean?' asked Niko.

'Gerhard chips all his animals,' said Robyn. 'He doesn't just track their health, he tracks their location –'

'So he will know exactly where this lion was killed,' said Ralph. 'Who else but us could've brought it down out here? Mbato's soldiers will come looking . . .'

'And our tracks are everywhere,' Grant realised.

'We need to get to the truck and fix it, so we can get away,' said Roland. He grabbed a tyre jack from the back of the jeep then swung himself into the driving seat. 'Everyone aboard. Now.'

The note of cold urgency in his father's voice made Ralph feel sick as he climbed back into the jeep. Roland started the engine, Niko got in beside him, and Robyn had barely climbed in next to Grant before the jeep jumped into reverse. Ralph fastened his seat belt as the vehicle rattled over the rocky terrain, crashing over the broken branches as they backtracked along the path Niko had carved out through the trees to escape the cave lion. Then Roland accelerated onto the route through the thick undergrowth that would lead them to the truck.

Suddenly the jeep lurched to the left, its wheels losing traction. Looking out the window, Robyn shouted, 'Mudslide!'

'Hang on!' Roland steered into the skid, the jeep's tyres chewing on thick mud, which spattered against the windows like blood as he fought to keep control. The squawks of terrified birds mingled with the roar of the engine as the vehicle slewed around in a half circle and slammed into trees, each impact sickening. Then the engine puttered out, leaving an eerie silence broken only by the cries of distant animals.

'Damn the rain,' Niko said.

Grant groaned in exasperation. 'Is nothing on our side?'

'*Nothing* is *exactly* what's on my side,' Robyn said hoarsely, holding herself statue-still. 'No sudden moves. We're on a precipice.'

Carefully, Ralph craned his neck to look around. Trees drooped away from them, their thick earthy roots displayed in candid tangles. The level ground had been swept away in the avalanche of mud, rock and vegetation, leaving a steep but navigable slope leading down to a wide riverbed, stony brown with a strip of glistening water running through its middle. Wildebeest and impala that must have gathered there to drink were now sprinting away from the unnatural commotion.

'Well,' said Roland quietly, watching them run. 'At least the going will be easier down in the valley.'

'But not in this,' said Niko, leaning out of the passenger window. 'This tyre's toast.'

'We can get out this side,' said Ralph. He opened the door on the right and carefully led the way out. 'Guess we'll have to reach Xai on foot.'

'No need. Xai has come to *you*.'

Ralph jumped, then relaxed with a smile as the familiar short, stocky figure of Xai stepped out from behind a red bushwillow, his rifle lowered to his side. The deep wrinkles in his weathered face owed as much to laughter as to age.

'Hey, Xai. Guess you heard us coming, huh?' Ralph said.

'Not for nothing were my tracking skills so highly valued in Ballantyne's Brigade,' Xai said drily. Then he placed a hand on Roland's shoulder. 'We need to get back to the truck. Developments.'

'Right,' said Roland briskly, handing him the tyre jack from the jeep. 'The rest of you – clear out the jeep. All our equipment. Eat something, then follow on.'

As the two men disappeared into the bushveld, Grant looked uneasy. 'Something's happened. Why are they leaving us out of it?'

'They won't for long,' said Robyn. She crossed her arms and frowned, staring after their dad and Xai. Ralph saw the frustration in her posture as clearly as if she'd yelled at them.

'She'll see to that,' Ralph agreed.

'I guess Xai has reasons for not telling us all here,' Grant said, like he was trying to convince himself. Ralph knew that Grant hadn't had such an easy childhood; the poor guy had fessed up to being closer to his nannies than his parents: his dad had been so focused on building the Green Freedom Party into a major political force that he didn't have much time for bonding with his son. Grant didn't share the same unconditional trust that Robyn, Ralph and Niko had in Roland and Xai.

Carefully, Ralph opened the trunk. Their equipment amounted to three hunting rifles with sights; a few rounds of ammunition; a revolver; a depleted first aid kit; the last of their field rations; a petrol can half-full of diesel; and three satellite phones with dead batteries. Ralph picked up one and cradled it carefully. In its sleeping memory was the precious video footage they'd taken of Mbato hunting a giant crocodile monster – proof that South Africa's big-game-hunter president was actively involved with Gerhard's sick schemes. Proof enough, Ralph hoped, to prompt a probe into Mbato's private affairs – and enough scandal to bring him down ahead of the upcoming election. Beyond that, though, the phones were useless; Gerhard had a whole flock of communications satellites in geosynchronous orbit over his land and the surrounding area, suppressing all signals. Even if the phones had battery, their group had no way of contacting the outside world or finding out how far the virus had spread.

'Kids,' Niko called. She was clearing confetti bush leaves from the glovebox – they'd been using them as deodorisers, with limited success – and stuffing them into a trouser pocket. 'Chow time.'

'Wild sorrel. Again. Yay,' Ralph said.

Robyn sighed. 'What I wouldn't give for a veggie burger.'

In his expansive office in the Union Buildings in Pretoria, President Julius Mbato sprawled back against the butter-soft leather of his chair, fingers tracing the fine woodgrain of his desk. He hated situations getting out of his control. Gazing around at his surroundings was usually a way to centre himself, to remind himself of his status and achievements. The matching bookcases held books chosen to impress. The comfortable armchairs placed on the richly patterned carpet had held the backsides of allies and enemies alike over the years: politicians, dignitaries, journalists, all trying to court him, or negotiate, or plead for his support.

Over the last several days people had poured in and out of the office, preferring to stand while bringing him bad news so they could escape his presence more quickly. They had brought news of the spread of the mystery virus. The spread of civic unrest. The spread of panic.

You're in charge, he told himself. *You're in control. No one and nothing can take that away from you.*

There was a knock at the door and his assistant entered. 'I've brought you the latest polling forecast as requested, sir.'

Mbato glanced at her, not moving from his comfortable position. She hesitated a moment then placed the tablet on his desk, where the bright glow of multicoloured opinion graphs contrasted with the smooth, heavy blackwood.

Only after she had retreated across the plush carpet and out of the presidential office did he pick up the tablet. He frowned at the infographics. The Green Freedom Party's numbers were improving and his personal ratings had dropped sharply. Typical of the whining, ungrateful masses. As if this damn virus sweeping from South Africa around the world was down to him!

No. It was down to Gerhard.

Mbato's fingers slowly closed into a fist. His partnership with Gerhard had been a profitable one – the man's money and manipulations had helped Mbato get into office, but had brought obligations and temptations. The binding ties that once had dangled so pleasingly now felt garotte-tight around Mbato's neck.

Gerhard's price for propping up Mbato's presidency was for Mbato's government to sell Gerhard a good chunk of the Kruger National Park. Fine. He'd agreed. But then Gerhard had sought more concessions to fuel his ambitions, offering Mbato so much in return: to hunt and kill his homemade monsters through his private grounds . . . and then to do the same to his political opponents too.

He's played you, Mbato thought. *Tapped into your greed for power*. Now they were steeped in so much blood, it was impossible to break clear. And all Mbato's compromises and betrayals and murders would be for nothing if he couldn't clean up Gerhard's mess.

His phone buzzed softly. Mbato looked down at the message, which came with no name or number attached.

TARGETS LOCATED. AUTHORISE STRIKE?

Mbato typed two letters.

Go.

3

Chewing on peppery leaves, Ralph and Grant followed Niko and Robyn as they trailed Roland and Xai to the truck. The sultry heat of the day curled about Ralph's body like rising smoke. Since the mudslide, the tree cover had grown dramatically thinner. He gazed up overhead, scanning for Gerhard's drones, which were surely on their way by now, and felt horribly conspicuous.

'The truck's on the other side of this thicket,' Grant said, gesturing past a clump of stunted knobthorn trees.

Suddenly a loud, harsh voice barked from the undergrowth ahead – a voice Ralph didn't recognise.

'*So many dead,*' it snapped. '*And it's spreading, isn't it?*'

Robyn passed one of her rifles to Niko. Ralph checked the revolver was loaded – his extensive safety training made the moves automatic. Then, as one, they crept forward through the undergrowth. But Roland heard them even over the static.

'It's all right,' he called. 'It's only the handheld radio.'

Ralph frowned. 'But Gerhard's been suppressing all communications.'

'Satellites can't stop Ham radio broadcasts,' said Xai quietly. 'They rely on antennae and repeaters. Use different frequencies.'

'Whoever's broadcasting that must be close by, for us to pick him up on the handheld,' said Ralph.

'Got to go,' the voice from the radio went on. 'Family needs me. Out.'

Ralph emerged from the thicket and stared around the small clearing. The voice had stopped; now only the static hissed and crackled. Roland leaned against the truck, fiddling with the handheld radio. The vehicle was facing away from Ralph: jacked up at the rear, it listed forward, poised precariously as if ready to crush the little crowd of saplings clustered before it and slither down the steep, muddy slope towards the riverbed. Xai lay in the mud, working busily underneath the truck to make the repairs.

Roland gave up on the radio, which still hissed and warbled its symphony of wavelengths. 'Was that the same voice, Xai?'

'Same as I heard while you were gone,' Xai confirmed. 'That's why I was on my way to fetch you.'

'Who was that?' Robyn demanded. 'One of Mbato's mercenaries?'

'We used to serve in the Recce with someone who runs a tourist lodge here,' said Xai. 'A man called Yonker. Up in the mountains.'

'Does it sound like him?' said Robyn.

'I think it does,' said Roland.

'But can he help us?' said Niko.

'Yonker's technically retired, but he's still available for special operations.' Roland looked at Niko. 'When we went to Pretoria to try to find out what had gone down in Gauda, we heard he'd been involved.'

'And is he involved in trying to find us now?' asked Robyn.

'It seems they've contacted him again, yes,' said Xai. 'There's a pandemic brewing and everyone's left his resort.'

'So, he's got nothing better to do than hunt down his old comrades?' said Ralph bitterly. 'Great.'

'It's an opportunity for us,' said Roland stoically. 'By listening in on his transmissions, we can learn the enemy's position –'

Niko shushed him. 'Listen,' she said. 'That's not just static from the radio . . .'

Robyn and Grant looked puzzled. But Ralph could hear it too, growing louder over the birdsong of the bushveld. A rising, whirring noise . . .

'Dad,' he said, licking his lips. 'I think we've got company!'

There was a sudden deafening roar of engines. Something huge and dark rose up in front of them from the riverbed: a large military helicopter in camo colours, gleaming in the sunlight. Two camera drones soared through the air above, filming the action as rotors whipped up a storm of dust. Blinking grit from his watering eyes, Ralph saw a gunner making ready in the cockpit.

'Take cover!' Roland roared as the chilling rattle of a machine gun cut through the chaos. 'Gerhard's found us!'

As gunfire tore through the air, Ralph threw himself under the truck beside Xai. The saplings ahead of them danced and splintered in a hail of bullets. Niko screamed and Grant shouted and the truck rocked above Ralph as people climbed in, accompanied by a chorus of metallic ricochets.

'Ralph!' came his father's shout. 'Xai?'

'We're all right,' Xai shouted back. 'Ralph, give me your rifle.' He snatched the Krieghoff Classic 'Big Five' double from Ralph's grip and rolled out from beneath the truck, cocking the rifle as he went. Xai fired both barrels to the helicopter, and the discharge rang in Ralph's ears. The wind grew less fierce as the chopper pulled away. Crawling on his elbows to peep past Xai, Ralph saw that Roland was out of the truck too, sheltering behind the driver's door and firing his own rifle through the open window, driving back their attackers.

'Get in, Ralph!' Robyn yelled, throwing open the rear passenger door. Ralph scrambled out from under the truck and Robyn and Grant pulled him in. Niko was sheltering in the footwell. Ralph lay beside her, grateful as her hand found his and squeezed tight.

'What do we do?' Grant shouted.

'We get the hell out of here.' Xai kicked the jack away from the rear left of the truck, which dropped down with a crunch. More bullets spat from the chopper's cockpit as Xai dived into the passenger seat. Roland was already in and gunning the engine. Ralph scrambled into the middle of the back seat. Through the mud-splattered windscreen he could see the ungainly shape of the large helicopter arcing up into the air away from them, ready to bank around for a second pass. Then the truck lurched forward with a metallic scrunch as it left the other jack behind. Trying to stay calm, Ralph grabbed the seat belt and buckled up as they plunged down the side of the valley on the jumble of soil and debris from the mudslide. They bumped so hard over the terrain that Ralph was sure the truck would flip and somersault, crashing onto its back and sledging the rest of the distance. But somehow the tyres kept their grip, and Roland managed to avoid the thickest trees, carving a great skid into the muddy sand of the riverbank before straightening up. They accelerated away, skipping over the floodplain, the shimmering strap of water running to their left.

'Hope you finished those repairs,' Grant said.

'So do I,' said Xai, as Roland accelerated. 'I guess this is the proving run.'

Robyn helped Niko to sit between her and Grant as the helicopter swooped away, parting company with the drones that lingered overhead. 'Where's the copter going?'

'It'll be scouting the way ahead,' Roland reported. 'Trying to anticipate our movements so they can radio back-up to cut us off.'

'That chopper is an Oryx,' Xai remarked. 'Manufactured by Denel Aerospace Systems for the South African Air Force.'

Ralph pulled a face. 'So?'

'So, this attack isn't black ops,' Roland explained. 'That copter may be crewed by mercenaries instead of regular troops, but it makes the mission official. Sanctioned by the president, funded by the public.'

Niko swore. 'Mbato just declared war on us.'

Ralph felt his chest tighten as he thought through the

implications of this. Mbato wasn't keeping his pursuit of them a secret any more, wasn't afraid of people knowing that he was hunting the Ballantynes. 'After two weeks drawing a blank, he and Gerhard must be desperate for results.'

Grant nodded. 'So, now they're chucking everything at us.'

'Only they're not,' said Roland. 'The Mitrailleuse d'Appui Général light machine guns on that helicopter can fire a thousand rounds per minute up to a range of eight hundred metres. They could have cut us to ribbons back there if they'd wanted to.'

'This isn't a private operation any more,' Niko supposed. 'There's accountability.'

Grant nodded. 'And if it ever comes out that Mbato ordered three kids to be shot in the run-up to the elections, that's gonna harm his chances.'

Ralph's mind raced. It was like having the goals for a game change halfway through a level. 'Do we think, then, that Mbato wants us alive?'

No one answered. But all the faces around him were drawn and doubtful.

Ahead of them the helicopter was coming in low towards them again. Through the open doorway of the brutal-looking aircraft, Ralph could make out the gunner lining them up in his sights. The machine gun roared into life once more. Ralph's eyes widened in horror as a line of impact explosions tore up the riverbed in front of them. They were driving headlong into the hail of bullets!

Roland wrenched the wheel hard to the left and the truck turned to avoid the rain of death. Ralph bit his lip as his dad stamped on the accelerator. Straight ahead of them now was a dead leadwood tree that had fallen in the mudslide and collapsed across part of the riverbank. The only way to avoid it was to drive back up towards the forest. But that wasn't an option.

'Hang on!' Roland yelled.

They hit the slope with an impact that seemed set to shake the teeth from Ralph's head. For a moment they were airborne, then they slammed back onto the ground with another bone-jarring impact. As they landed, the truck lurched to one side. For one heart-stopping second, Ralph thought they were going to topple over. At the last moment the truck righted itself and, with a cry that was half rage and half triumph, Roland changed gear once more and the truck raced towards the forest.

'The copter's still coming!' Robyn shouted.

Ralph could practically feel the thud of the rotor blades as the helicopter closed in behind them. Then the air was filled with the death-rattle roar of the machine gun as it opened fire yet again. Grant and Niko screamed in terror as bullets battered the back of the truck. Roland started to weave the truck wildly from side to side. The treeline bumped painfully closer. Cover. A chance to hide.

We're going to make it, Ralph thought, hope rising.

Then there was a loud bang and the truck dropped at one side. Above the roar of the engine Ralph could hear the *thwack-thwack-thwack* of torn rubber beating against the underside of the truck. The bullets had burst at least one of their tyres. The tailgate banged open and equipment tumbled out – rations, rifles, ammo, a petrol can.

'We're losing everything!' Grant yelled.

Ralph swore as the drones dropped in altitude, closing in. *And the next thing we lose is our lives.*

'All right, listen!' Roland yelled as the listing truck began to slow. 'I'm going to stop. Ralph, Robyn, Grant – take the phone with the predasaur hunt video and run for the forest. Xai, Niko – we'll hold them off.'

Ralph gripped the phone in sweaty hands. 'You won't stand a chance!' he said, his voice cracking.

'We won't leave you,' Robyn told her father. 'We can't.'

'We'll deal with them and then we'll come find you,' said Niko.

Roland threw a look over his shoulder as he stopped the truck. 'You've got this, guys. I trust you.'

Ralph swallowed hard. He had wished so many times to hear these words from his dad. But not like this. Never like this.

The forest was tantalisingly close, but the helicopter was even closer. Ralph held his breath as the noise of the twin turboshaft engines grew until it drowned out everything else. He closed his eyes, waiting for the sound of the machine gun to join the cacophony.

It didn't come.

The helicopter was landing on the flat riverbed, turning its rear towards them. 'Protecting the cockpit,' Ralph reasoned numbly. 'Heavy-duty cargo doors are more resistant than a cockpit, even an armoured one –'

The clunk of the truck door opening cut him off, and his dad's bawl made him jump. 'Robyn, *no!*'

His sister had jumped out and was sprinting towards the supplies that had tumbled out of the truck. Grant hesitated for a moment, then bolted after her, ignoring Niko's shouted order to wait.

Ralph made to follow, but Roland shouted at him. 'Ralph, *stop*!' Such was the authority in his voice that Ralph froze instantly.

Xai finished loading the rifle he'd taken from Ralph and held it back out to him. 'Take this, Ralph. You'll have to help us cover those two.'

Ralph stepped out, using the rear door as cover just as Xai had. He saw that Grant, an excellent sprinter, had already caught up with Robyn and was trying to pull her back.

She shook off his hand. 'Grab some equipment,' she ordered. 'We stand no chance without it. Go!'

'Rob, Grant, get back here!' Ralph shouted desperately. He gripped his own rifle in sweaty hands as a metallic clank from the copter's cargo bay made his insides quail. The drones fanned out around the copter. The heavy door slowly swung open from the top, ready to create a ramp down to the damp sand.

'Back, *now*, you two!' Roland yelled. He and Xai jumped from the vehicle and took up defensive positions behind the truck's battered bonnet.

But either Grant and Robyn couldn't hear or they didn't want to; she was racing for a box of ammo and he for the rifle that would fire them.

'Do we surrender?' said Niko.

As the cargo bay ramp struck the sand, Ralph imagined himself and the others captured by the troops, prodded inside its dark depths like animals.

Then he saw that the animals were already inside.

Two bright red eyes appeared. A colossal, cat-like shape slunk cautiously into the sunlight, its broad nose sniffing the air. Each paw was the size of a dinner plate. A second giant beast emerged behind it, its neck and shoulders rippling with muscle. Then a third padded out. The long, curved fangs of the three giant beasts glistened with drool.

With a deep stab of terror, Ralph realised they were facing a pack of sabre-toothed tigers.

4

Robyn clutched the box of ammo to her chest, frozen in horror. In Gerhard's compound she'd found herself trapped in a cage with one of these red-eyed monsters and she'd barely survived. Now she was facing *three*. Her instincts screamed at her to turn and run – instincts that had been part of human make-up from ancient times. *Mbato's men don't have to fill us with bullets,* she realised. *They can stay safely on board while they let these creatures rip us apart.*

As the drones whirred overhead like vultures, the predasaur sabretooths prowled and twitched, their red eyes narrowed. The nearest threw back its huge head and gave a rumbling, throaty growl. Robyn forced herself to meet the beast's stare, to try to reach out to it. To empathise. Usually, the connection she felt with wild animals bordered on spiritual. She had even befriended two lion cubs as a child, and the bond of mutual trust and protection between them endured to this day: Robyn could read each flicker of emotion in their amber eyes. But these sabretooths were more than Ice

Age animals reclaimed from extinction. They were vehicles of pain, rage and appetite, engineered by Gerhard for one purpose – to kill, and preferably on camera.

'Grant, Robyn, get down,' Roland bellowed behind them. 'You're in the line of fire.'

She caught movement from the corner of her eye. It was Grant, throwing himself to the ground. His elbow struck the petrol can with a clang and it toppled onto its side. Precious fuel spilled from the broken cap, sucked in greedily by the earth.

No! That's all we have spare – we need every drop! Robyn couldn't help herself – she ran to grab the can and set it upright.

At the same moment, the nearest sabretooth ran too. Straight at Grant.

The beast was a savage blur of ivory teeth and corded muscle. Time seemed to slow. Gunfire cracked out. The predasaur took a hit, blood welling from a wound in its neck, but the impact barely fazed the giant cat; it was too big, too angry to stop. Robyn dropped the box of rounds and fell to the earth beside Grant. As the sabretooth bore down on them, she grabbed the fallen can and swung it with all her strength against the beast's face, splashing petrol into its red eyes. Crazed, the creature thrust its head forward, ready to bite Robyn's own head clean off. Terrified, she held up the fuel can in front of her face to protect herself. The predasaur's fangs clamped down, twisting and piercing the metal. With a growl of anger the sabretooth recoiled, the canister wedged between its jaws, petrol splashing everywhere.

Damn it! Robyn thought.

The sabretooth's reaction spooked its two brothers; they reared up and skittered backward as more bullets began to fly.

Grant rolled over and snatched up the ammo that Robyn had dropped. She got up too and saw a white plastic box she didn't recognise embedded in the soft mud beside her. She stooped, grabbed it, and ran with Grant for the shelter of the truck. A blood-curdling roar filled the air and she pushed herself faster. Ahead of her she could see Xai, Niko, her dad and Ralph ranged around the truck, their firearms at the ready. She ducked but kept up the punishing pace as they started to fire past her.

'Keep going,' Ralph shouted. He fired then winced as the recoil shunted at his shoulder. 'Come on, Rob!'

With a last despairing push, Robyn threw herself under the rear passenger door like a base runner sliding into home base in the last innings. Niko crouched over her, but not to check she was OK. Instead, she twisted free the white plastic box Robyn still clung to and opened it.

Flare pistol, Robyn realised. She watched for a few seconds as Niko, who knew the dangers of South Africa's wildlife, having treated patients up and down the Crocodile River, calmly but swiftly took the bright orange pistol and loaded a cartridge from the clip attached to the handle.

Propping herself up on her elbows, Robyn dared to check on the tiger-beasts. And what she saw chilled her. At first she thought the two sabretooths had ganged up on the one with the petrol can jammed in its jaws; tigers were solitary creatures, they didn't do well in groups. But no. They were *helping* their brother. Heedless of the bullets smacking into the side of the helicopter, the beasts were biting and swiping at the dented canister with their heavy paws to free their fellow sabretooth.

It was unnatural. But then, so were predasaurs. And if they felt like part of a pack, perhaps they sensed that they would have more success working together.

'Why are you guys wasting ammo on the copter?' Grant panted, joining Ralph behind the door. 'Those monsters are the target!'

'Take them out and we're still left with all the troops on board.' Ralph took the loaded flare pistol from Niko. 'When we saw you'd picked this up, we changed tactics . . .'

'*Got it*!' Roland yelled over him. 'Now, Ralph!'

Robyn followed her dad's line of sight, and saw fuel spilling from two bullet holes punched in the helicopter's hull. Then she understood the change of plan. Ralph pulled back the trigger and the flare fired with a hot popping sound. It sizzled into life just as it hit the side of the chopper. The aviation fuel caught light immediately, and fire rained down. With a *whoomf* the petrol on the ground ignited too, splashed all around by the sabretooth, and a wall of flames sprang up. Soldiers shouted as the inferno took hold around them, but the agonised roars of the big cats cut through Robyn's heart. Her whole life had been about protecting animals. She sobbed at the pain the sabretooths were feeling, but their enemies had left them no other way to escape. Through the curtain of flame and smoke she saw one blazing sabretooth roll in the mud and sand to extinguish the flames, while another ran to the water. The third took down one of the soldiers and tore into his struggling form in a frenzy, even as it burned.

'Robyn, get inside.' Niko was helping her up. 'You're drenched in fuel. If one spark catches you . . .'

Without warning, the helicopter exploded. A crimson fireball bloomed from clouds of thick black smoke, engulfing the drones. Grant pushed Robyn into the back seat of the truck and Roland shouted, 'Everyone in!' Fiery debris clattered down around them as, with a harsh grinding of gears, the truck crawled forward once more, lurching wonkily with its flat tyre for the treeline. Robyn lay on the sticky leather, listening as the sound of crackling flames and the mournful drawn-out wail of a sabretooth finally faded into the distance.

In his private office suite, Josef Gerhard stared at the flames flickering over his 3D virtual display screens. By blinking through his smart glasses he could make any one of the smaller screens go supersized, filling the wall with high-def images. But right now, there was nothing but fire.

Through the now-stationary camera of one of the downed drones, Gerhard caught the shadow of a sabretooth limp past, dragging a soldier's mauled body. It was a bleak, apocalyptic image. Interesting that the big cats had shown primitive reasoning in their efforts to dislodge the petrol can from their brother's jaws; an unnatural loyalty to their kind had overcome the expected instinct to kill. Perhaps predasaurs felt united by their difference from the native wildlife. That would certainly make them more formidable hunters – and more formidable prey.

Gerhard froze the action with a blink and went back through the recorded footage to take a screenshot of the tiger with its haul of burnt flesh. *Yes*, he thought. It would make a good cover for a future *Predasaur* game. No one would ever know it was taken from real life, just as no one suspected that the *Predasaur* cut-scenes were adapted from real murders. Gamers enjoyed realistic violence, and Gerhard was a firm believer in giving the paying customer what they wanted.

It was a shame the drones had been damaged in the explosion. An obliterated helicopter with its surviving crew being subjugated by sabretooths would make for an entertaining spectacle. And without eyes in the sky – or another predasaur with tracking chips like the cave lion finding the scent – he had no way to follow the Ballantynes. The idiots should've been dead ten times over by now, yet they clung on to their miserable existence.

Still.

Gerhard hurled his lead crystal glass at the floor, where it shattered into a thousand glittering shards, each reflecting the vivid flames displayed on the wall of screens. It was as though glowing embers were trapped in every speck, raging to break free. Gerhard forgot his anger, entranced as ever by the beauty that bloomed from violence and his own natural skill in creating it.

A gentle alert sounded from his call screen. Gerhard took a breath and pulled his gaze away as he tapped the Accept key. For a moment he caught sight of his reflection in the glass before the powerful features of Julius Mbato filled the screen.

There was no smile or word of greeting. 'The strike was successful?'

'No. The helicopter has been destroyed,' Gerhard said simply.

'What?' Mbato leaned forward angrily. 'And the assault team?'

'Half of them were burned alive, and more will become cat food. Judging by the drone footage, I don't think there will be more than two survivors.'

The heavy line of Mbato's pursed lips ran parallel to the furrows in his forehead. 'Each of those mercenaries was paid in advance,' he hissed. 'And I had to pull that Oryx from scheduled medevac missions in Gauteng Province. Questions will be asked about why its crew detail was taken off roster.'

'Surely,' said Gerhard, 'with this virus spreading through the population so rapidly, changes in air force personnel fit to fly are to be expected.'

'*This* virus?' Mbato slammed his palm down against his desk. 'It's *your* virus. It's spreading around the globe, turning into another pandemic, and the pathogen came from *your* predasaurs. Thanks to you, the only chance I have of winning this election now is by flattening the death count curve. You need to make a cure for me.'

'I often wish there *was* a cure for you,' Gerhard muttered.

Mbato's eyes narrowed. 'If you want all South African tech firms using computer chips engineered by Gerhard

Industries – chips I know you'll load with enough malware to open every system, cripple your competitors and expand your empire exponentially – you need me in power for a third term . . .'

'And without my company's chips inside the country's vote-counting machines to rig the results, you won't get one.' Gerhard smiled. 'So we're both still useful to each other. My scientists are making good progress developing the cure at the secondary complex. I predict a breakthrough soon –'

'Soon?' Mbato broke in. 'May I remind you that the elections are only three and a half months away!'

Gerhard felt irritated at Mbato's lack of patience. He always looked for the quick fix when he should be planning more carefully instead. 'Surely you can delay them, given the circumstances?'

'My critics will accuse me of a power grab,' said Mbato, frown lines deepening on his forehead. 'The usual dull accusations of corruption and excess. And if Ballantyne manages to send that evidence of me hunting predasaurs in your game reserve to my competitors before we've prepared a plausible explanation . . .'

'On that point, at least, I think immediate action can be taken,' Gerhard announced. 'In times of terror, people need a focus for their frustration and fear – and I can give them one. As the virus goes on spreading, and as fresh lockdowns bite, let's see to it that Roland Ballantyne dominates the headlines – for all the wrong reasons. We'll have the entire world baying for his blood.'

'Destroying Ballantyne's reputation is no substitute for destroying the man himself,' said Mbato. 'We can't let them slip off the radar again.'

'They were heading north-east – hoping to lose us in the mountains, perhaps.' Gerhard smiled. 'But that territory holds secrets known only to me . . . and it has hidden dangers that I can exploit.'

Mbato looked thoughtful. 'I know the area too. We fought there together, Roland, Xai and I, just before I was forced to leave the Recces.' A smile curled about his lips. 'I believe I can call upon some local assistance to help with our cause.'

Gerhard raised an eyebrow. 'Oh, yes? What sort of "local assistance"?'

'You'll see,' said Mbato. 'You're too busy looking to the future, Gerhard. You neglect your past.'

'Meaning?'

Mbato smiled. 'The strength of a successful leader is forged in youth – and in a crisis, that strength can be called upon.'

'Is that a fact?' Gerhard purred. 'Well, then, by all means, summon your assets from the past. The more the merrier. Let our traps close around Ballantyne and his clan – and crush them all.'

5

In the truck, the atmosphere was tense. Grant had his eyes closed, pretending to sleep. In truth, he was so exhausted he longed for sweet oblivion, but the eyes of the predasaurs burned on in his memory.

Roland and Xai had fixed up the shot-out tyre with the remaining jack as best they could in a remarkably short time. The tyre pump had been lost when the tailgate broke open, but that didn't stop them. While Xai dug out resin from an acacia tree, which he used to seal the puncture in the tyre, Roland rigged two Schrader chucks onto a siphon hose. By connecting one end of the hose to the flat tyre and the other to the pumped-up tyre at the front, the pressure equalised, leaving both tyres with just enough air to function.

Niko and Ralph had gone foraging for food, and found the scavenged remains of an eland antelope – enough to butcher for rations, at least. Robyn and Grant took an inventory of the kit they had left. It wasn't a long list. Grant gave Roland the bad news. Roland only grunted in response.

'Thanks,' said Xai, and Grant imagined his smile was meant to be reassuring. It wasn't.

Grant wandered off back to Robyn, sitting now in the shade of a tree. 'Your dad's mad as hell. You'd think he'd be grateful for what you did.'

'Yeah, well. Dad doesn't approve of me having a mind of my own.' Robyn wiped angrily at her eyes. 'But I guess he has a point. I led Ralph and Luke into Gerhard's reserve, even though they didn't want to come. And Luke never came out, did he?'

Grant groped around for something comforting to say. But he had nothing. He kept quiet.

The repairs took less than an hour, then it was back on board the truck for the next stage of the journey. With their position exposed, stealth was no longer possible. They had to hope that Xai's people were out there, and they would offer shelter and help.

The truck rumbled along a narrow stretch of rocky hillside, hemmed in on either side by euphorbias creating a rim around the skyline. The trees, with their inverted umbrella-like crowns of branches, looked like eerie prehistoric sentries, barring them from the cover of the wider forest. It wasn't just the damaged tyre that was making the truck ride so uncomfortable either; Roland was still giving Grant and Robyn the silent treatment.

Grant knew what it was like to have a father who gave his all to a cause. As leader of the Green Freedom Party, Max Khumalo demanded loyalty from all around him, family included. No – family especially. For Grant, that had been way easier in his younger days. His mum had died when he'd been just a baby, which had driven his dad deeper into his political work. Grant remembered him as a kind presence, but a distant one. Schooled and cared for by a succession of nannies, Grant had learned that the surest way to get his dad's attention was to excel in class or to take an interest in ecological matters, and so for years he had done both. But then, having developed an enquiring mind, Grant felt compelled to experiment – and found he got a lot more attention from his dad (even if it was negative attention) when he signed up for the Winter School for Young Hunters and attended shooting competitions. It had felt good to think that his actions could still have an effect on the old man.

He opened his eyes and looked at Robyn. Her head rested against the window. Tentatively, he tapped her hands. She jumped, looked at him like a startled okapi.

'Sorry,' he said quickly. 'I just wanted to say . . . thanks. You know. Back there.'

Robyn shifted uncomfortably. 'Don't mention it.'

'Yes,' Roland said curtly. 'Don't mention it.'

Grant frowned. 'Why are you angry, Mr Ballantyne? We wouldn't have got away without Robyn.'

'I gave you an instruction.' Roland's voice was quiet, which was somehow way scarier than if he'd been shouting. 'Robyn disobeyed, and jeopardised both your lives.'

'This isn't the army, Dad,' Robyn said hotly. 'I'm too old to follow your orders blindly.'

'Speaking of blind,' Ralph broke in, trying to change the subject, 'we still haven't seen any sign of your people, Xai.'

'The Bakho,' Xai said. 'That is the name of my people.'

'You said you didn't know the name of the tribe that lived here,' said Robyn, taken aback.

'The elders did not wish our name to be known,' Xai explained, 'in case that too was taken from us by those in power.' He paused. 'The Bakho lived in harmony with these lands – until the mining corporations moved in. Now the landscape has changed beyond all recognition, and I fear the Bakho have moved on. That is why our search has been unsuccessful.'

'Because Mbato's government decided that metals beneath the earth were more important than those who lived off it,' Niko added, frowning. 'Relocated most of them to shanty towns on city fringes. Changed their way of life.'

'The Green Freedom Party pledges to overturn those rulings,' Grant said firmly. 'We'll put things right. The people will return.'

Xai smiled sadly. 'It's too late, my friend. The mining companies have ripped the heart from our homelands. There's nowhere for the people to return *to*. Yet I still hope that we may find isolated groups clinging to the old ways. Living carefully, secretly.'

Robyn took a deep breath. 'Like us.'

'Doing what they must,' Xai agreed, looking between Roland and Robyn. 'Finding new ways to get along.'

In the rear-view mirror, Grant saw Roland catch Robyn's eye. She smiled just a little, and Roland smiled back. Xai nodded, apparently contented.

The truck rumbled on, picking up speed as they moved

out of the forest and back towards the dry riverbed that they had originally been following.

'Why aren't we staying under cover?' asked Grant in surprise. 'Surely the forest will give us a far better chance of staying hidden.'

'The trees are also hiding us from the sun,' said Xai. 'Now that we've lost our fuel supply, we need to make sure we keep the truck's solar batteries topped up.'

There was no accusation or reproach in Xai's voice regarding the loss of the fuel. It was merely a statement of fact. Grant knew that the truck's V8 400hp diesel combustion engine was backed up by two powerful electric motors. The batteries that ran them were charged either when the diesel engine was being used, or via the solar panels on the cab roof.

'In any case,' Xai added. 'We have to cross the valley sooner or later.' He pointed towards a distinctive rocky outcrop shaped like a bird's head silhouetted against the sky on the mountainous ridge across from them. 'I recognise that peak. It marks the start of an old poachers' trail.'

'It's where we saw action all those years ago,' Roland said. 'With luck it should still be passable.'

'And from there I stand a better chance of finding the way to some of the old settlements,' Xai added.

'Perhaps we'll find a clue to where the people went,' said Grant, 'if nothing else.'

Once they had crossed the riverbed and started to climb, the terrain quickly began to change. Trees started to become more and more scarce and the lush grasses of the valley gave way to thorn thickets and scrub. The track they were following became far more rugged too, littered with rocks and boulders that had rolled down the slopes from the jagged outcrops above. As the sun started to edge lower in the sky, their progress slowed to little more than a crawl. The mountainside on one side of the track was getting steeper by the minute, and the drop on the other even more so.

When it was dark, Roland parked; they couldn't afford to wear down the battery by using the headlights. Xai found a small clearing and Grant helped him build a fire. Ralph and Niko put together a spit over which they roasted gristly strips of antelope, which Robyn had cut from the carcass with Xai's pocketknife. While they worked, Roland napped in the truck.

'Wish I could sleep on command like that,' Grant remarked.

'You learn to, on covert operations,' Xai told him. 'Got to stay alert. Fresh.' He sniffed his own armpit dubiously. 'Mentally, if not physically. Being out here again . . . it takes me back to those days.'

'When you were with Special Forces?' Ralph asked.

Xai nodded sombrely. 'Our unit was based out of Phalaborwa.'

'Back then, Mbato fought with you,' said Robyn, joining in with the story. 'Not against you.'

'Our great president was in your unit?' Grant was surprised. 'As well as that guy you heard on the radio – Yonker?'

'That's right,' said Roland quietly from the truck.

'What happened?' Grant asked.

'If it's the story I think it is,' said Robyn, 'then Angel Abrafo happened.'

'Abrafo,' Ralph echoed in a theatrical whisper, picking the last meat from the blackened skin of the antelope.

'I'd like to hear this story,' Grant said.

'I'm not sure you would.' Roland stepped out of the truck, stretched and sat down beside the dying fire. 'But all right. I'll tell it to you.'

6

'It's almost twenty years since Xai and I were here last,' Roland said. 'Our brigade was assigned to capture a high-value target – Angel Abrafo, head of a notoriously vicious gang of poachers and animal traffickers who took high-risk, high-reward jobs for wealthy clients.'

Xai nodded. 'Abrafo's lot had no hesitation about killing anyone who proved an obstacle – rangers, local villagers, even children. They'd caught dozens of rare species and shipped them out of the country to be trophy pets. And they'd killed scores of rhinos for their horns and elephants for their ivory.'

Roland took up the litany of crimes. 'On one occasion they stole into a protected reserve at the foot of the Klein Drakensberg with a commission to take the ivory from seventeen bulls. They didn't realise that the elephants' tusks had already been removed for their protection, so there was nothing of value left to take. Abrafo and his gang chose to slaughter the elephants and take their ears back to their paymaster to prove they did the job and were entitled to be paid for it, ivory or no ivory.'

'Scum,' Robyn muttered.

'And they operated here in the mountains?' Grant asked, looking all around with a shiver.

'Yes. Sifting through reported sightings by locals, we determined the likely location of Abrafo's base as somewhere on Mount Mananga,' Roland said. 'So we set off on a loaded march for forty-three miles through tropical forest and savannah. I felt we stood a good chance of locating our targets before they could move against us.'

'Mbato marched behind me,' Xai recalled. 'He was the odd one out in our unit. Quiet, didn't joke much with the rest of us. But there's no denying he was an expert shot, particularly at long range.'

Roland nodded. 'Whenever I needed a sniper, Mbato was my go-to. He outranked me – he'd climbed to warrant officer, whereas I was only a sergeant – but in the Special Forces it's a man's mission experience that gets him command.'

'So, he was above you on paper but in the brigade you called the shots,' Niko reasoned.

'Interesting,' said Grant. 'I'm not saying that Mbato running for president, the biggest guy in charge, was him massively over-compensating, but . . .'

'You'd be right,' Ralph agreed and they grinned at each other.

'Anyway.' Roland sipped a capful of water from the caddy about his neck. 'There we were, moving through a ravine, thinking we could use the tree cover to get to our next vantage point and overlook Abrafo's camp. But somehow Abrafo knew we were coming. His men were waiting for us, hidden among the ironwood and ebony trees. They opened fire without warning. I'm only here now because Xai dragged me down into the cover of the understorey.'

Xai looked into the darkness, the fire reflected in his eyes. 'Three of us were cut down in the ambush – Yonker, Gazi and Mbato. I saw Gazi get shot, and his lifeless body fall to the ground.'

Grant broke in, puzzled. 'Yonker and Mbato?' But Robyn shook her head at him, and he swallowed the interruption.

'Two more, Simmons and Antony, made it back along the ravine. But the poachers followed Xai and me.' Roland looked into the dying fire. 'I took down one of them and Xai shot two more before we reached the shelter of the ironwoods. They came after us. I couldn't even call for back-up; my radio had taken a bullet in the ambush. But we smeared our bodies in mud to deaden our scent and hid out up a tree, in the thick leafy branches. Eventually the poachers gave up looking for us.'

'Abrafo's men must have thought us weakened, diminished, no real threat,' Xai said. 'As poachers, they should've known – never underestimate your prey. Even a wounded buffalo will circle back on its pursuers and strike without warning.'

'Once we'd tracked Abrafo's men back to their camp higher in the mountains, we watched and waited from a vantage point in the rocks,' said Roland. 'And then Antony and Simmons were dragged in. They'd been captured.'

He paused. Grant looked around the campfire. Niko was held rapt by the story, while Ralph and Robyn looked solemn. They'd heard the story before, of course. They knew what was coming.

'Abrafo wanted to know who'd informed on him, who had made it possible for the Special Forces to find him,' said Xai. 'Simmons and Antony wouldn't say. So he told them he had an informant of his own in the Recces, and that he needed to teach our commanding officer a lesson for daring to send troops after him.'

'And with that Abrafo shot them, at close range in cold blood,' said Roland softly. 'Men I'd loved as brothers – murdered right in front of my eyes. I reached for my gun, hot for revenge. Ready to put down Abrafo. But Xai stopped me.'

'Good for Xai,' said Niko in a low voice.

'The camp was too heavily guarded for us to do anything on our own,' said Xai dully. 'We'd be throwing our lives after our friends'. What kind of vengeance is that?'

'The little rogue was right, of course. And we knew where Abrafo kept his base now. We could launch an aerial strike. Take out Abrafo's entire gang. End him for good, even if that meant missing out on the intel we'd get from interrogations.'

'Exhausted as we were, it still only took us forty hours to get back to base camp,' Xai remembered. 'There we found out that Mbato had survived after all and beaten us back. He looked shaken to see us, for a moment – almost afraid, as though we were ghosts – and then he recovered and was all smiles.'

'He claimed he'd faked being hit by the bullets to trick the poachers. Then he'd managed to crawl away to cover. Thinking we were all dead, he made his way back to the nearest town.' Roland took another sip of water. 'I asked, did he know what happened to Antony and Simmons? He told me they'd been killed in the initial ambush with the others, and he'd gone back and checked their bodies. And he said he'd overheard a hunting party say they'd bagged Xai and me.

'Of course, we called him out on this in front of our commanding officer. Antony and Simmons were still alive when he claimed to have found their bodies. But Mbato stuck by his story. Just said in the confusion he must have taken Yonker and Gazi for Antony and Simmons. I said that was bull. Abrafo knew we were coming, because Mbato must have tipped him off. It was the only explanation: he'd sold out his regiment for blood money from South Africa's most notorious poachers.' Xai shrugged. 'He denied it, of course.'

Roland nodded slowly. 'An airborne operation was already under way to hit back at Abrafo, but it was too late. He'd gone to ground, ready to do his filthy work elsewhere. We took Gazi, Simmons and Antony back home, but at least it wasn't too late for Henrick Yonker. We found him, barely alive. Badly wounded, but he'd managed to get away too.'

'Yonker was never the same again.' Xai shook his head. 'He quit soldiering not long after that. We lost touch.'

'The whole brigade was torn apart,' said Roland. 'And there wasn't enough evidence to bring Mbato to court martial, so the whole thing was hushed up and he left the service. Xai and I retired the following year to set up Crocodile Lodge . . .'

'And it was around then that I saw Mbato in a bar surrounded by cronies,' said Xai. 'Drinking the kind of champagne that went nicely with the flashy Mercedes parked outside.'

'Blood money from Abrafo,' Ralph muttered, 'for ratting you out.'

Roland nodded. 'And that money must have bought Mbato some powerful friends, because the next time I saw him was five years later, on the news, climbing the political ladder with the African National Alliance.'

'He got massive campaign donations from Josef Gerhard, in exchange for special "favours" when he reached office.' Grant remembered his dad talking on the subject. 'Such as buying two thousand square miles of the Kruger National Park from the government, dirt cheap, so Gerhard could have his own luxury hunting grounds.'

'And a base for his sick experiments,' Robyn added.

'Well, that's what we've got to prove to the outside world,' Roland said. 'When we get there.' He stood up and kicked dirt over the last embers of the fire, leaving a weak moon as the only light. 'In the meantime, we should all try to rest up.'

'There could be more predasaurs,' Robyn murmured. 'Out there in the dark.'

'I'll take first watch,' Ralph said.

'Four hours, then I'll take over till dawn,' said Xai. Everyone nodded. Roland and Xai climbed into the front of the truck while Niko clambered heavily into the back, looking dead on her feet. She left the door open, then looked

54

back at Grant and Robyn. With a small smile, she pulled the door shut.

Grant rose, stiff from sitting on the hard earth, and offered Robyn a hand to help her up. She raised an eyebrow as if to say, 'Really?' and got to her feet by herself. Then she shook his hand jokily. 'Hi, I'm Robyn,' she said quietly. 'I'll be your fellow insomniac in the stinky truck of doom.'

'Pleased to meet you,' he whispered back. 'At least while you're wide awake you won't snore.'

Robyn frowned. 'I don't snore!'

'You're like a warthog with asthma,' Grant informed her.

'Well, you smell like one,' Robyn countered. She tugged on his shirt, the ghost of a smile on her lips. Strands of hair blew across her face in the night breeze. Her face looked softer than he'd seen it before.

'I've heard that when things are like this . . .' she said quietly. 'You know, dangerous, intense, each-minute-could-be-our-last kind of stuff . . .'

Grant looked into her eyes. 'Adrenaline through the roof, that sort of thing?'

'Right. I've heard that can sort of affect your feelings and . . .' She grimaced. 'I dunno. I'm good with understanding animals, but people? Ugh.'

'I reckon a lot of people don't even understand themselves,' Grant found himself saying. 'Especially when there's so much going on and no time apart and . . .'

'Yeah.' Robyn seemed to shake herself awake. 'I guess you're right.'

'Or not!' Grant cringed inside. He'd been trying to

sympathise, but felt somehow as if he'd just shoved Robyn away. 'I mean, people should, you know, definitely think about . . . stuff.'

Robyn nodded and turned to the truck. 'Yeah. Night, Grant.'

'Um, right. Night. Night!' He groaned out loud as Robyn climbed into the back seat beside Niko. *Smooth, Grant*, he thought, as he got in beside her and closed his eyes. *Real smooth.*

Robyn listened to Grant's breathing, trying to work out if he'd given in to sleep. Then she heard him swallow and shift. She was glad she wasn't the only one replaying the conversation and peeking through her fingers at the different directions it might have led.

You're crazy, she told herself. *Feelings only complicate things. Stop you thinking straight. Tomorrow we could all be dead.*

Was it wrong to want to clutch at any chance to be happy?

As the night animals croaked and chirruped, Robyn fell into troubled dreams about running through a maze of dark corridors. She kept finding belongings from her bedroom at the lodge scattered around, like a trail leading her to something unknown, something that scared her more and more the closer she came to finding it.

She never did. Instead, the rattle of gunfire made her burst awake in the muddy light of dawn. The truck was rocking gently, as if they were moving, yet the engines were dead. A hissing noise, like air escaping in a rush, made Robyn fear that the tyres had been holed. But the sound was shifting about, and a shout carried over it. Xai's voice – he must be outside on sentry duty, which meant that Ralph must be in the passenger seat . . .

'*It's got you! It's right around the truck!*'

Ralph, Grant, Dad, Niko were all suddenly awake, staring around in confusion. The windscreen was covered with what looked like a sheet of textured fabric – leather or rubber of some kind. It was only when Robyn looked closer that she saw the fabric moving, flexing, *undulating* . . .

'What *is* that?' gasped Niko from beside her.

Ralph jumped back from the front passenger window as something thick and heavy slapped against the glass. Red eyes in a huge, serpentine head glared in, unblinking, as the truck rocked harder. With a shock of horrid clarity, Robyn realised that the 'fabric' on the windscreen was in fact the pale, ribbed hide of some enormous reptile, whose body was wrapped tightly around the truck.

'Snake!' Xai screamed, opening fire again. 'It's a giant monster snake!'

7

Ralph felt frozen inside – not just with horror but with sheer disgust. He'd played all the versions of *Predasaur* and knew at once what this thing had to be – not just a giant snake but a titanoboa, a hideously large killer from Earth's prehistory. Fifteen metres long and weighing more than a ton, it was a recurring big bad in *Predasaur* boss levels. Ralph relived in a rush so many gory scenes he'd played, believing them to be animation. Now he knew the truth – that Gerhard enhanced real footage of his monsters killing people that he and Mbato considered their enemies, selling slaughter as entertainment. Ralph wondered if drones were filming the super-snake winding itself around the truck right now, ready to crush it like a tin can to reach the prey trapped inside.

Roland had managed to lower the passenger side window enough to get an arm out and had opened fire with the revolver, but the bullets seemed to have no impact on the creature's flesh.

'That thing's head is on the left of the truck!' he shouted. 'Try to get out on the right.'

'It's jammed,' Grant shouted as he kicked furiously at the door.

Ralph kicked and hammered at his own door. It was no good. Instead, the titanoboa seemed to squeeze harder and the door began to crumple inward. Ralph glimpsed a flash of movement past the bulk of the beast.

It was Xai. He charged boldly up to the titanoboa, shouting wildly, and clubbed it repeatedly with his rifle; had to be out of ammo, thought Ralph. There was a hiss that sounded like a million cans of Coke opening and, with a spasm of rippling flesh, an obscenely thick tail struck Xai and he was sent tumbling into the brush.

'Xai!' Roland shouted.

At the same time, the creature slackened its vice-like grip on the cab, shifting position in the murky dawn light. Roland switched on the truck's headlights. Ralph gave a gasp of horror as he got a better look at the thing they were up against. Its tubular, diamond-patterned body was thicker than a barrel and its blunt, arrow-shaped head was the size of an oil drum. The titanoboa let out another hiss of anger, opening its mouth to reveal long fangs. As its mouth opened, Ralph could see its quivering pink gullet. A thin black vertical pupil slashed through each blazing red eye. The snake reared back . . .

Then struck.

Ralph threw himself to one side as the scaly head smashed through the front of the truck, buckling metal and shattering the windscreen, showering everyone inside with glass. Niko shrieked and slid down in her seat, trying to stay out of the predasaur's reach. Meanwhile, Roland attempted to aim the revolver at the snake's eye, but the monstrous head was thrashing to and fro and he couldn't get the shot. Robyn pushed both legs between the front seats and tried to kick at the titanoboa, beating at the scaly bulk of its head as if hoping to drive it out of the truck. The snake lunged at her, jaws widening, and Roland launched himself at its head. Gripping the inside of the snake's mouth between its fangs, he struggled to hold apart the beast's upper and lower jaws so it couldn't bite.

'Shoot it,' he grunted, shaking with the strain. 'Weak point, down the throa—'

But that weak point flexed and twisted back. Ralph screamed, and so did everyone else in the truck, as the titanoboa wrenched Roland out of his seat and flung him through the air like a doll. He hit the ground and rolled head over heels through the undergrowth.

Robyn cried out. At first Ralph thought she was crying for their father, but then he saw that she had snatched back her leg; a deep bloody gash ran through the flesh. But there was no time to help her. The snake had pushed its great head inside the truck again, probing the air with its thick, rubbery tongue, eyes like red searchlights zeroing in on its prey. Grant grabbed the other rifle and struck the snake in the face with the stock, while Niko clambered into the front seat and slashed and stabbed at its eyes with a broken windscreen wiper. Maddened with pain and bloodlust, the snake began to twist and turn wildly, and a jagged ivory fang got hooked through the steering wheel and jammed there.

The predasaur strained to get free, but only managed to twist the entire steering column upward. Now it couldn't push forward into or withdraw from the truck, further hampered by the jagged glass edges of the shattered windscreen slicing against the thick flesh of its neck.

'Quickly!' Ralph yelled. 'While it's stuck, everyone out now.'

Grant forced open the rear passenger door and scrambled over the serpent's body. Niko managed to clamber out through the driver's window, and Grant helped pull her through while Ralph tried to manoeuvre Robyn outside.

'Dad,' she said. 'Where's Dad? And Xai?'

Ralph shook his head helplessly. 'I don't know, I didn't see.' As he worked out how best to help Robyn, he winced at her bloody wound. 'How's your leg?'

'Hurts like hell,' she said through gritted teeth. 'That thing must've bitten me.'

'It's more likely broken glass,' Ralph told her, and prayed it was true. He couldn't think of a constrictor that was venomous in the natural world, but the dark vertical pupils were a feature of venomous snakes; it would be just like Gerhard to make his monster even deadlier than the original. 'Anyway. Whatever got you, we need to stop the bleeding . . .' He struggled to support her as he stumbled outside, then he gasped as something grabbed hold of his arm.

Spinning around, Ralph found with relief that it was only Xai, sporting a swollen, bloody bump on his forehead. With Xai's help, Ralph guided Robyn away from the thrashing bulk of the snake with calm precision.

61

The truck rocked harder as the titanoboa struggled to free itself. Niko broke free of Grant's steadying hold and ran to Xai.

'Where's Roland?' she asked. 'That fall he took . . . He could be unconscious, or maybe he broke something . . .'

'We'll find him. I'm sure he'll be fine,' Xai promised.

'Will Robyn be?' Ralph murmured, as he and Xai propped his sister up between them.

Niko steadied her breathing and bent to inspect Robyn's leg. 'It's a deep gash.' She jumped as the truck beside her was dragged a whole metre away from them through the mud as the titanoboa redoubled its efforts. 'Damn it, the first aid kit's in there!'

'*Everything's* in there,' Ralph groaned.

'We'll carry you to higher ground, Rob,' Grant said, taking her feet as Xai took her shoulders. 'Get you somewhere safe so Niko can check you over properly.'

Ralph felt a flash of resentment at the older boy trying to take charge of his sister. But he knew Grant was right. He hurried along beside them with Niko, scrambling up the rise and past thorny brambles, out of sight of the giant serpent. Carefully, Grant and Xai placed Robyn down in some long grass.

'Niko,' Xai said, producing a roll of bandage and a pack of adhesive plastic strips from the pocket of his field vest. 'I have DermaClips to close the wound, but should we apply a tourniquet first to stop the bleeding?'

'Yes, definitely.' Niko took the bandage and wrapped it around Robyn's thigh, about five centimetres above her knee.

Xai passed her the plastic strips. 'You've used these field stitches before?'

Niko nodded and her eyes focused for the first time since the snake attack. 'Place over the wound, pull to join the skin and clip off the tabs.'

Ralph knew what Xai was doing: he could easily have applied the first aid himself, but he was trying to keep everyone occupied with their own mission. To stop them going into shock or fearing the worst for Roland.

'Ralph,' Xai said. 'Find a stick for Niko to use as a windlass to tighten the bandage –'

'Grant can do that,' Ralph said. 'I'm gonna help you find Dad.'

Xai looked about to argue, but then there was a rattle of gunfire from further down the slope, beyond the truck.

Grant froze, staring at Xai in alarm. 'Is *that* Roland?'

'That was an automatic weapon,' Ralph said, gulping. 'Dad only had a pistol.'

Niko looked up frantically. 'There must be someone else down there!'

Further gunfire barked its idiot song. With a chill, Ralph realised it was coming from more than one weapon.

'More of Mbato and Gerhard's little helpers?' Ralph hissed.

With a screech of tearing metal and the crash of breaking glass, the titanoboa finally pulled itself free of the truck. In a fluid, sinuous movement it reared up into the brooding sky, and through the brambles Ralph caught his first proper look at the beast in its entirety. It was a terrifying sight, nearly ten metres longer than he had estimated. Its eyes blazed with primal hatred as it turned and slithered away down the slope, rivulets of dark blood leaking from cuts in the diamonded hide below its jaw.

'What is that thing doing here?' Ralph whispered. 'You don't hunt snakes. Not even enormous ones like that.'

'If it was reared to be hunted, it wouldn't be bulletproof,' Xai pointed out.

Ralph nodded. 'Then Gerhard made it for some other reason.'

More automatic weapons rattled into life.

'Let's take a look at what's happening,' Xai said. 'Carefully.'

Ralph followed as Xai set off stealthily, climbing up the hillside. The morning sky was dark with clouds rimmed with sun fire, even as fat drops of rain started to spatter around them. Although he was careful, Ralph was painfully conscious of the loose rocks and stones he dislodged beneath his feet as he climbed. He prayed that the noise that they made as they clattered down the rockface would be drowned out by the sound of gunfire and the angry hissing of the titanoboa. As they crested the hill, Xai held a finger to his lips. Moving as silently as he could, Ralph crept forward to join him. Brushing the wet hair from his eyes, he found himself looking down into a valley that branched off the main trail, its entrance blocked by boulders. Behind the boulders, at least six men were firing as the enormous serpent slithered towards them.

'No uniforms,' Ralph noted. 'Can't be army . . .' Then

his jaw tightened as he looked beyond the boulders and noticed a figure lying prone in the back of a truck even more battered than their own, parked between a couple of Land Rovers. A man with a bruised and bloodied face, his hands zip-tied behind his back.

'Dad,' he breathed.

8

'Roland's down,' Xai muttered. 'They must have found him when he was thrown down the hillside . . .'

The titanoboa lunged, cobra-fast, towards its tormentors. The men fell back, but one was too slow. The terrifying serpent clamped its jaws around the man's torso, its fangs biting deep into his flesh. Screaming in agony, the man was lifted high into the air. With a flick of its head, the snake swallowed him whole. To his horror, Ralph could see the writhing, struggling shape of the man caught in the snake's throat. For the briefest moment he thought he could hear muffled screams, before the sound of gunfire drowned out all else.

'Fall back!' The hoarse order rang out. The men jumped into their vehicles, which roared into life. A man in a denim shirt and a bandana crouched over Roland's body.

Panic clutched at Ralph's chest. 'They're taking Dad.'

'Regroup at Boulder Pass!' Bandana Man shouted. 'We'll send someone for Rontane and Tharn when they've got the rest of them!'

Dread trickled through Ralph's thoughts like the raindrops down his back. *Got the rest of them?*

But Xai's reaction was stronger; he actually flinched. 'Kali Rontane,' he said. 'The so-called Queen of the Poachers.'

'You know her?'

'By reputation. Came up through Angel Abrafo's gang. Soft as a rattlesnake. Twice as deadly.' Xai watched intently as the pickup and the Land Rovers jerked away from the line of boulders, slipping in the wet mud as they reversed over the rough terrain. Ralph braced himself, waiting for the titanoboa to slide over the boulders and pursue its prey. But it didn't. It stared after them, swaying from side to side. Then it turned and moved away, its bulk churning through the wet mud as the rain fell harder.

'All right, come on.' Xai started to walk away. 'We have to get back to Niko, Robyn and Grant. If Rontane's after us . . .'

'But those guys must be poachers, not soldiers,' Ralph said. 'They wouldn't work for Gerhard?'

'Mbato has ties to poachers in the region, remember? And Kali Rontane is as brutal and ruthless as her old boss.' Xai spat in the grass. 'Her and Abrafo are outsiders even within their own sick community. They're capable of anything.'

Ralph nodded. He knew the grim statistics: that on average forty elephants each day were murdered for their ivory. The money from the illicit ivory trade was a source of funding for organised crime, and it made ten billion dollars a year.

'Do you know the pass they were talking about?' Ralph asked.

'I think so. We can track the tyre marks they've left, in any case.' Xai's face was creased with worry. 'So long as the truck isn't too badly damaged.'

'We have one rifle left,' Ralph said, 'and we're practically out of ammo. But at least the titanoboa's gone.'

They climbed quickly back down the slope, making for the little clearing where they'd left Niko, Grant and Robyn. But then a woman's voice rang out from lower down the hillside. 'Xai! Xai?'

Ralph froze instinctively, and Xai immediately dropped, dragging Ralph with him.

'I know that you and the Ballantyne boy are out there, little rogue. Come on out . . .'

Ralph sensed Xai stiffen at her mocking use of his old military nickname. 'She knows you.'

'She's been briefed,' Xai murmured, and slithered silently towards an overhanging ledge edged with knobthorn.

Ralph crawled after him. Through the thorny barrier he could see Robyn on the grass, her bloodied leg stitched up, Grant crouched protectively beside her. Then he spied a stranger: a man in a black T-shirt and shorts, cradling a high-calibre hunting rifle with a silencer in his arms, stood over them. That had to be Tharn. A few metres away Ralph saw a tough-looking woman in a green vest, camo jacket and a baseball cap. That could only be Rontane. A similar rifle was slung across her chest and an ammo belt hung around her waist – and she had a pistol placed to Niko's temple.

'Your freak of a serpent killed one of my men, Xai.' Rontane sounded casual but Ralph could see she was peering all around, alert to danger. 'I'm entitled to take a life in exchange.'

'What does she mean, *our* serpent?' Ralph hissed.

'She's trying to get a reaction from us,' Xai murmured.

'It's you and the Ballantynes we want. The others don't matter. I'll kill the woman first, then the boy.'

Ralph could practically feel the fight go out of Xai. He knew that they had no choice; they had to surrender. When they'd had the element of surprise, they might just have had a chance, but now the advantage was with Rontane.

'All right,' Xai called. Turning to Ralph, he lowered his voice. 'Maybe I could say you ran away and –'

'We can't take that chance,' Ralph said, heavy-hearted. 'If she doesn't believe you, she could kill Niko *or* Grant and still have a hold over you because she'd still have Robyn. But why does Rontane want us?'

'I'll give you one guess: Mbato.' Xai nodded. 'He's dealt with Abrafo before. When we moved on from Gerhard's territory, he must have put the word out. The poaching community knows the territory better than anyone.'

'They didn't seem to know about that giant snake on the loose,' Ralph said with a shudder. He wondered again: Why did Rontane think the monster was anything to do with them – and where had the predasaur come from? There'd been no sign of giant serpents in Gerhard's game reserve. But all these questions fled his mind as they rounded an acacia tree and came face to face with Rontane and the others.

Up close, Rontane looked even more formidable – a big, tough-looking woman with two gold front teeth shining in a mouth of stained yellow. The gun she pointed at Niko's head had clearly seen plenty of action. Grant stared grimly at the barrel, as if hypnotised. Robyn sat a few metres away with Rontane's comrade, Tharn, standing over her. Her leg wound had a neat line of plastic strips over it, the tourniquet was still wrapped around her thigh, and she was pale.

'Put the gun down, Rontane,' Xai said. 'We're not armed.'

'More fool you,' said Rontane. 'Call it in, Tharn.'

Tharn raised his rifle and coughed loudly and noisily. His sallow face was beaded with sweat as he spoke into his phone, using a dialect Ralph couldn't decipher.

'Your friend seems sick,' Niko said slowly. 'Has he been to any urban areas lately?'

'You think this is funny?' Rontane jammed the revolver's barrel harder against Niko's head. 'Think you and your lover-boy are clever?'

'D'you see us laughing?' Robyn scowled. 'We should get away from here before that giant snake –'

'*Your* giant snake.' Rontane stared at her coldly. 'I'm a man down, thanks to you. He was a lazy waste of space, sure – but you'll pay.' She looked across at Tharn. 'Ironic, huh? Us doing a public service for once. Maybe our beloved president will give us a medal as well as the bounty.'

Xai was losing patience. 'Look, we've told you. We don't know what you're talking about.'

'Tharn downloaded the Channel Two news report in Pretoria so we'd be able to recognise you,' Rontane said. Waving the gun, she gestured Niko and Grant over to Ralph and Xai. 'Go ahead, Tharn. Show them.'

Tharn stabbed at his phone screen. He held it out in his left hand, keeping the gun trained on Robyn in his right.

Roland Ballantyne's face appeared on a screen behind the news anchor Ralph had seen on Channel Two a thousand times before. A chill ran down Ralph's back.

'Evidence has come to light that a respected authority on wildlife conservation management, Roland Ballantyne, has been funding genetic research into bringing extinct animals back into the wild – with deadly consequences. We warn viewers that this news item contains images that some may find distressing . . .'

Robyn, straining to see the screen, scowled. 'What the –'

Tharn coughed noisily. Xai held up a hand to silence him, frowning at the screen. Lazy raindrops began to fall again, splashing on the screen as if the sky was crying.

Ralph could barely believe what he was seeing as the 'story' unfolded. The footage and images had been faked or taken out of context to create a brand-new narrative. The report claimed to show that Roland Ballantyne had recreated savage beasts from prehistory (cut to shots of the sarcosuchus, the cave lion and a woolly rhino) by inserting ancient DNA into modern animal cells to rear predators and prey. Ralph recognised Gerhard's lab, but it appeared to be Roland's face behind the surgical mask. Then the voiceover detailed how Roland's son and daughter had used cutting-edge software developed by Luke van Rok, heir to VanRok Security Solutions, to smuggle the creatures onto Josef Gerhard's reserve as an anti-hunting stunt to damage Gerhard's standing (cue a montage of shots that chilled Ralph.

There was security camera footage of himself, Robyn and Luke running through Gerhard's reserve, then the cave lion attacking a security guard). The news anchor continued that Grant Khumalo – son of the Green Freedom Party's founding leader Max Khumalo – was aiding their criminal trespass. The screen now showed Grant with a rifle watching hippos being attacked by cave hyenas. Apparently Ballantyne himself, his former adjutant, Nqosa Xai, and his partner Niko Haart, a professor of epidemiology and expert in zoonotic diseases, had later stormed Gerhard's reserve themselves, killing ten rangers as they ran amok. The footage showed Xai and Roland shooting at Gerhard's rangers, who staggered and fell, then the shot cut away to show Niko smashing a Crocodile Lodge jeep into one of Gerhard's trucks.

Ralph's mouth hung open in disbelief. 'It didn't happen that way . . . none of it!'

'Sure,' said Rontane. 'We believe you. Totally.'

Just when Ralph thought it was over, the twisted narrative went on. Experts were convinced that the new virus spreading through the world was not only zoonotic but from ancient animals – and that it had flared up in South Africa. The implication was clear: the Ballantynes were to blame for Gerhard's virus.

The piece ended with a statement from President Mbato. 'I served with Ballantyne and Xai in the Recces twenty years ago,' he said. 'Many of his men died during Ballantyne's watch on an anti-poaching operation that led to his eventual resignation from the service. I believe this tragedy has led to his desire for vengeance against *all* hunters.'

'Anyone who could pick up a gun and kill a defenceless animal needs to be stopped.' Roland's face filled the screen. 'They deserve to die.'

'He never said that,' Xai muttered.

'It's a deepfake,' said Ralph. 'Gerhard has enough computing power to create fake footage like that. Most people will believe that without questioning it.'

Finally, pictures of all of them were shown and the news reporter continued. 'These fugitives must be considered highly dangerous. If sighted, do not attempt to approach or engage. Call the police at once.'

The report cut off, and the screen faded to black.

9

Robyn was gritting her teeth so hard that her jaw throbbed. But she was damned if she was going to cry in front of Rontane and her pet thug. To imagine the whole world watching reports like that! Her dad's reputation and future had been blown away in a handful of deep-faked moments.

'All right, Tharn, let's tie their hands and move out.' Rontane smirked. 'Ballantyne's always acted so pure and innocent and holier-than-thou. But all along he's been sick in the brain.'

'It's bull!' Robyn snapped.

Tharn prodded her shoulder with the butt of his rifle, indicating she get up. 'Move.' He coughed noisily in her face and she turned away, disgusted. 'Move, or you're gonna be sorry.'

'I'd save your breath, Tharn,' Ralph told Tharn. 'Sounds like you haven't got so much of it.' He helped Robyn to stand and she winced with pain.

Grant took her other arm to steady her. 'They've royally

screwed us,' he muttered. 'Discredited your dad *and* mine by association . . .'

'And Luke,' Ralph whispered. 'Poor Luke, what will his family be thinking now?'

It's my fault Luke got involved, thought Robyn. *All of this is my fault*. 'The whole world will be against us now.'

'Explains why Mbato felt able to send that Special Forces helicopter after us,' Xai said.

'Lucky for my bank balance, we found you first.' Rontane held Robyn's wrists together in front of her and slipped plastic zip-ties over them, pulling them tight. 'Don't worry too much, though. It's all good. The army will mop up your pet monsters and the land will be safe again – safe for us to do our jobs, at least.'

'Jobs!' Robyn glared. 'That's what you call the slaughter of incredible animals? A job?'

Rontane shook her head, smiling. 'I call it a vocation.'

The rain started to fall harder. Under Tharn's baleful gaze Rontane tied Xai's hands together, then Grant's, Ralph's and Niko's. A squawk came from Tharn's radio. He wiped his forehead and muttered into the radio before reporting to Rontane. 'No snake in sight.'

'Good. We'll move out.' She straightened her wide-brimmed hat, protecting her face from the downpour. 'May as well take the Ballantyne truck so there's room for all the bodies. I'll take Xai, Khumalo and Niko in that. You take Ballantyne's kids.'

Rontane pushed Xai and Grant towards the truck, keeping a tight hold on Niko's arm.

'Robyn,' Niko called, 'you mustn't leave the tourniquet in place. Take it off when you're lying down.'

But Tharn was already herding Robyn and Ralph ahead of him in the opposite direction, down a sketchy path through the brush. Still the rainstorm battered down on them. Robyn was soaked through in seconds. Ralph lost his footing and slid, cracking his shins painfully against the sharp rocks, but Tharn just laughed and hauled Ralph to his feet. He was looking all around as he walked, gripping his gun tightly, watching out for the serpent.

Robyn limped through the long grass and edged closer to Ralph. 'Looks like this is game over,' she said quietly. 'Catching us will make Mbato a hero – bagging dangerous terrorists who probably unleashed this virus on purpose.'

'The report didn't say that,' Ralph argued weakly.

'They made damn sure to say that Niko's specialty is zoonotic diseases. The public will put two and two together –'

'And make five.' Ralph lowered his voice. 'But I still have the phone. There's the video of Mbato hunting the sarcosuchus on Gerhard's land –'

'Move faster.' Tharn shoved Ralph forward, and he nearly slipped again. Robyn gasped as she almost fell with him, but even with his hands tied he clung on to her and helped her navigate the densely wooded hillside.

'That video's worthless now,' Robyn muttered.

'You're right.' Ralph seemed to deflate. 'It's all been for nothing.'

They trudged on until they were walking past tangles of bushes, not trees, and a battered Land Rover came into sight.

Tharn pushed them on towards it. Robyn hissed with pain as thorns scratched at her bad leg. The skin around the wound was red and puckered, fresh blood mixed with rainwater dribbling down from it to stain her sock crimson. The gash would scar, for sure. Assuming she lived long enough for that to happen.

'In.' Tharn slammed Ralph against the wet door and gestured for him to open it. The tang of stale sweat and fetid leather greeted them. Ralph helped Robyn inside so she could lie on her back, elevating her bad leg. The rain beat a cacophony on the Land Rover's canvas roof.

'Niko said you should take off the tourniquet,' Ralph reminded her, getting in beside her. Robyn nodded, her tied hands fumbling with the stick that held the tourniquet tight around her thigh. Tharn got into the driver's seat, still coughing. Robyn cringed, her memory snapping back to her day in Gauda at the start of this nightmare, when she had helped Niko to treat victims of the virus. The rattle of coughing had been the soundtrack to that ordeal.

'I think he's caught it,' she hissed to Ralph, loosening the bandage. 'Gerhard's virus.'

Ralph swallowed hard. 'No, he can't have. It'll just be a cold, or a fever or something.'

But when Tharn turned and knelt on the driver's seat, staring at Robyn and Ralph past the headrest, Robyn could see that sweat dripped from his face and that his bloodshot eyes were red-rimmed. He still gripped the rifle in one hand, but had another set of plastic zip-ties in the other. He jabbed the gun butt into Ralph's legs, indicating that he raise them. 'Ankles, now. No tricks.'

Ralph glanced at his sister, then slowly raised his legs.

Tharn coughed again, a deep, hacking sound, without covering his mouth. Ralph cringed and turned away. Tharn put down the rifle while he fitted the zip-tie around Ralph's ankles and pulled it tight.

At that moment, Robyn sprang forward and looped her tourniquet around Tharn's neck, twisting hard. The poacher roared in anger, clutching at his throat. Thrashing about, he pulled away. Robyn almost lost her hold, but Ralph kicked out at Tharn's face, his muddy boots cracking against the man's temple, knocking him back into the dash. Robyn leaned forward, pulling on the ends of the bandage as if Tharn was a runaway horse she was trying to control. He was still groping around for his rifle, and finally his fingers found it. He tried to lift it, but Ralph kicked it away. Finally, Tharn stopped struggling and slumped against the steering wheel.

'Let go of the bandage,' Ralph gasped. 'You'll strangle him.'

Robyn had already released her grip. 'Don't leave the tourniquet on for more than ninety minutes,' she hissed at Tharn.

Ralph pulled the rifle from the front seat into the back. 'What are we going to do?' he asked Robyn. 'My ankles are tied and your leg is a mess. Can't see us getting far. Unless . . .' With some effort, he pulled a large folding knife from the poacher's trouser pocket. 'Sharp thinking?'

Robyn winced as much at the joke as from the pain in her leg. 'Just cut my hands free and I'll do the same for you.'

'Ladies first,' Ralph agreed. He pressed on a catch and the blade flicked out. 'Hold still.' He started to saw through the white plastic zip-tie on her wrists. 'If I cut through a vein or something . . .'

'You won't.' It came out as more of an order than a reassurance. Robyn softened her tone. 'You'll be careful, I know.'

But Ralph didn't move.

'What is it?' she asked.

'D'you hear that?' he whispered.

At first, the steady drum of the rain on the roof was all that Robyn could hear. Then there was something else: a strange sound, echoing distantly, as if coming from everywhere at once. It sounded like the sea, a noise like waves crashing against the rocks.

The realisation of what was approaching hit them simultaneously.

'Flash flood,' breathed Robyn.

It was, she knew, a common enough hazard in the mountains: when the rain fell so fast that it was unable to drain into the soil fast enough, roads could swiftly become rivers. Before their deadly hide-and-seek flight, this had seemed like abstract information, but the collapsed hillsides they'd witnessed and the boulders they'd had to clear on the road here showed just how powerful a flood could be.

'We need to get out of here,' Ralph said, starting to panic. 'Change of plan. You cut *me* loose and we'll climb up as high as we can.'

'I can't climb anywhere!' Robyn slapped her palms against her thigh and gestured to her wound.

'I'll carry you. Fireman's lift,' Ralph said, throwing open the driver's door and sliding out to stand on his still-tied feet. 'But I need to be able to walk.' He stooped and sliced viciously into the thick plastic restraints holding his ankles, grunting as he pulled them free. Then he shuffled stiffly around to open the rear door, the knife still in his hands. 'Come on.'

'Too late!' Robyn shouted: through the filthy rear windscreen she saw a wall of water surging down the road, set to engulf them. 'Ralph, get in,' she snapped. 'Now!'

Ralph was already moving, hurling himself inside as the water struck the Land Rover, hard as a giant sledgehammer. The car skidded forward, and Robyn and Ralph were thrown off the seat in a tangle of arms and legs. Freezing cold water stung her skin as the deluge lifted the Land Rover off the ground entirely and they were swept down the hillside, spinning about as if they were on some nightmare funfair ride.

'Brace yourse—' Ralph shouted, but his words were choked off as filthy water poured in through the open passenger door, soaking him. Robyn's wrists were still tied and her left leg was agony so she could only use one knee and her back to wedge herself in place in the footwell. Their speed increased with every passing second, and there was a sickening scrape of metal on stone as they hit something. They crashed into a tree and the windscreen caved in as the tree branches forced their way inside, like thick, thorny fingers questing for prey. For a few seconds the splintered wood anchored them there.

'Rob!' Ralph shouted, sitting up in the flooded footwell. 'You OK?' He looked like a drowned rat as he sawed furiously at the zip-tie around her wrists. 'We gotta get out –'

More water hammered down on top of him as the Land Rover jerked forward again and the canvas roof was torn open by the tree branches. Again, they were pitched into freefall. As Robyn was thrown backwards, the zip-tie snapped and her wrists were released. But then the Land Rover tipped over onto its side, bumping and scraping over rocks as it was carried along in the torrent. Robyn shrieked as she tumbled over the back seat and struck Ralph, pinning him to the door.

Then the Land Rover hit something else with a deafening bang and righted itself. The rear end swung out into the floodwater and the door flapped open.

Robyn clung to Ralph as the two of them were thrown from the Land Rover into the filthy, frothing water. For what felt like forever, her world was literally turned upside-down as the flash flood engulfed her and Ralph. Every few seconds she found herself able to snatch a breath as her head came to the surface, but then the current dragged her down again as the river of water, mud and debris swirled them around.

She choked back a cry of pain as the raging water poured into a crevasse, slamming her into the rocky wall. Ralph's wrists were still tied, so she put her arm through his to link them. He kicked and she front-crawled with her free arm as they tried to stay afloat. And despite the buffeting,

81

it was working. It was actually *working*, and Robyn felt hope begin to rise inside her.

But then they were swept against a protruding rock, and Robyn felt her brother go limp. His head dipped under the water.

'Ralph!' she shouted, trying to pull him back up as they were carried out of the crevasse and into a larger body of water. The mountain track had become a raging river and the powerful current proved too strong for her. Robyn gave a cry of despair as Ralph was ripped from her arms. She caught one brief glimpse of his motionless body before the torrent dragged him away.

10

Slowly, dizzily, Ralph woke from a terrible nightmare about drowning.

At least, he assumed it was a nightmare . . .

Yes, it must have been. Otherwise, how could he be back in his bed at Crocodile Lodge? At least, he *assumed* it was his bed . . .

He sighed and stretched. Of course it was his bed. It was warm and soft, and the sheets and blankets were tucked tightly around him.

But . . . why was his hair so wet? And his face?

Ralph opened his eyes. The fuzziness in his brain allowed only trickles of detail to get through, but he knew that something was wrong. If this was his bedroom, then the ceiling had been torn away. He was staring up at the remnants of storm clouds scudding across a deep black sky. *I remember something about a storm*, he thought uncertainly, and hoped Robyn and his dad were OK in their rooms. He looked around. His bedroom walls seemed to be missing too, and if this really was his bed then it was moving in the most peculiar way – squeezing, *tightening* . . .

As his last moments of consciousness came crashing back into focus, Ralph panicked. 'Robyn?' he shouted, and tried to get up. But he couldn't move his legs. He was stone-cold with horror. Had the battering he'd taken in the floodwaters left him paralysed? No, he could *feel* his legs, he just couldn't move them.

As he struggled to sit upright, straining to see what had pinioned him, the moon emerged from behind the clouds, and Ralph realised that the reality of his situation was worse than any nightmare.

Battered and bloody, the titanoboa had also survived the flash flood. Its eyes were barely a metre from his own and Ralph's legs were already deep inside the creature's gullet. With every passing second it was drawing him deeper into its jaws.

It took all of Ralph's willpower not to dissolve into a screaming panic. The giant snake was obviously injured, but it was still more than a match for him. Any sudden movement on his part would only kill him sooner.

I can't die, he told himself. *I've got to find Robyn.*

Ralph blinked furiously, willing his eyesight to sharpen in the moonlit gloom. He could see that the floodwater had deposited him in thick, wet mud at the bottom of a shallow valley. At least the zip-tie around his wrists had snapped at some point. All around him were boulders and uprooted trees. He spotted a truck wheel, then the twisted wreck of a Land Rover and assorted pieces of debris.

Must be Tharn's, Ralph figured. *Swept down here like I was.*

Ralph craned his neck to see if there was anything within easy reach that he might be able to use as a weapon. With a surge of hope he spotted a rifle, half buried in the wet mud. *Probably Tharn's too.* Keeping his movements slow and steady, he stretched out for it, but it was just out of his grasp.

He sifted through the mud, searching for something that he could use to extend his reach. If he could hook a branch or something through the rifle's strap . . .

Just then, he felt the pressure around his thighs increase, and he was jerked towards the snake, his fingers raking through the mud as he tried to find purchase. As careful as he had been, his movements had obviously alerted the snake to the fact that he had regained consciousness. Clearly, even weakened, it wasn't ready to lose a meal.

Realising that there was nothing within reach that could stop him being pulled into the snake's maw, Ralph changed tack. If he couldn't do anything to get away from the snake, then he needed to come up with a plan of attack for when he was *closer*.

As the creature's jaws slid over his waist, he jabbed his fingers hard into the creature's right eye. The snake gave a hiss of discomfort but showed no sign of releasing its grip on him. Ralph jabbed even harder, feeling the soft tissue squish beneath his fingertips. This time it had an effect. The snake writhed in pain, thrashing its head from side to side and shaking Ralph as if it was a child playing with a rattle.

Ralph gave a cry of pain as he hit something hard, half buried in the mud. It was a small fire extinguisher, which must have torn free from the Land Rover.

Knowing that this was his only chance, Ralph began to struggle, beating at the snake with one hand while scrabbling desperately for the fire extinguisher with the other. He moaned with fear. Twice his fingers brushed against the metal handle, but on each occasion he failed to get a grasp. Finally the snake's writhing brought him within reach and he got a firm grip on the handle.

With a wet sucking noise, the extinguisher came free. Yelling in triumph, Ralph pulled out the pin and unleashed a cloud of CO_2 into the snake's face.

The effect was instantaneous.

Convulsing, the titanoboa virtually vomited up Ralph before recoiling. Ralph blasted again with the extinguisher, splashing and sliding about as he tried to push himself away with his heels through the thick mud. The titanoboa gave up, and began to slither away. Clutching the canister to his chest, Ralph listened to the sound of its scales rasping across the ground as it glided off into the night.

For the next minute or so he just lay there, exhausted, barely daring to breathe, straining to hear the monster returning. But the night was eerily silent, with only a few mournful calls and caterwauls from the darkness, as if the bush were licking its wounds.

Ralph had more than a few of his own to tend to. First, mostly from habit, he felt inside his sock for the mobile phone with the evidence against Mbato filed away in its internal memory. It was still safe against his ankle, along with about a dozen bruises. He dragged himself over to the wreck of the Land Rover, hoping to find a first aid kit, but all he found was a mangled body jammed beneath the steering wheel. For a moment he was afraid it was Robyn. Then he saw the bandage around the neck and realised it was Tharn.

Ralph nearly hurled. He quickly abandoned his search, squelching and slipping over to perch on the trunk of an uprooted tree. He was wet, cold and exhausted. Every muscle in his body ached, and his arms and legs were a mass of cuts and bruises. All he wanted to do was curl up and sleep, but how could he? Robyn was out there somewhere. He had to find her. Then maybe they could track down their dad, and Niko and Grant and Xai, and rescue them from Rontane and her poachers before Mbato could . . .

For a moment the hopelessness of the situation almost overwhelmed him.

Almost.

Then he forced himself to get back to his feet. Giving up was not an option. He was a Ballantyne, and his family were relying on him. He was like his ancestor, Zouga Ballantyne, an adventurist, and he planned to stay alive to add his story to the family journal.

He began to look around the valley floor, sifting through the wreckage brought down by the floodwaters to see if there was anything that might be useful to him. Frustratingly, the rifle's barrel was bent, so it could never be fired again, but on impulse he unclipped the rifle's telescopic sight. That, at least, seemed undamaged, and it might come in useful.

He had more luck with food and water, finding a rucksack containing a full canteen and several foil-wrapped survival rations. Clearly Tharn was well used to the demands of long treks through the veldt in search of helpless animals to slaughter. Suddenly realising how hungry and thirsty he was, Ralph unwrapped one of the ration packs and wolfed down its contents. He took his time with the water, taking a couple of long, grateful mouthfuls before screwing the cap back onto the canteen and stuffing it back into the rucksack. There was no telling how long it might be before he found clean water again, so he needed to ration himself.

Ralph did one final sweep of the debris field but, apart from a foil survival blanket, he saw nothing else that would be of use to him. Packing the blanket alongside the water and provisions, Ralph hoisted the rucksack onto his shoulders and set off unsteadily into the night. Almost immediately he stumbled over a gnarled, broken tree root and fell flat on his face in the mud.

And he knew it then: fear was overriding all that his father and Xai had taught him. Attempting to search for Robyn in the pitch black South African night was madness – worse, it was suicidal. He was cold, he was wet and he had no light. In his current condition, there were a million ways that he could be killed, besides a grudge match with that giant serpent. He could come face to face with a hunting predator (and given the stink that his clothes were giving off, they'd have no problem tracking him) or he could fall into a ravine or river. Even spraining his ankle at this point would be catastrophic.

With sudden clarity he realised that he needed to find somewhere safe where he could dry his sodden clothes and could catch a few hours of sleep. By his reckoning the sun would be coming up in a matter of hours, and then at least he would be able to see properly whatever dangers he was facing.

Ralph came across a tree and clambered up it until he found a fork in the branches into which he could wedge himself without fear of falling. Satisfied with his refuge, he stripped off his wet clothes and hung them on the branches around him. He might not be able to get them clean, but he could at least try to get them dry.

Shivering in the cool night air, he pulled the foil survival blanket from the rucksack, unfolding it and wrapping it around and underneath him like a cape. As he leaned back against the tree he could hear the distinctive call of a fiery-necked nightjar ring out through the night air. Ralph took that as a good omen. The nightjar's chirruping cry was often described as 'good lord, deliver us' and just now he could think of nothing more apt.

But what was that humming, buzzing noise behind it, far off? Sounded like a helicopter . . .

Ralph's weary eyes flicked open. *Mbato's men again*, he thought. *They've found me.* He looked upward but the canopy of leaves hid the night from view – and him from eyes in the sky, he hoped.

The drone of the rotors faded like a dream. Ralph closed his eyes, listening to the nightjar repeat the phrase – *good lord, deliver us* – and within a minute he was asleep.

11

Robyn woke, shivering, to see daylight stretching through the shadows of a cave. But she wasn't cold. She felt hot, and a band of pain sat hard behind her aching eyes.

Through the cave mouth she could see a lush, green valley and a wide river fringed with trees, tall grasses and flowering plants. It was beautiful; so beautiful, her mind all but rejected it.

How had she got here? She remembered limping through the night for what felt like ages, but had that just been a dream? Her clothes were dry, she realised – and memory snatched her away to disjointed impressions of the flash flood. One of her last clear memories was of Ralph's lifeless body vanishing from view as the frothing water swept her away from him. After that, her recollections began to get hazy.

'Remember,' Robyn muttered, hugging herself tight. 'Focus.'

The flood water had whisked her down the mountain like a leaf carried along a gutter. She'd barely been able to keep her head above water. Finally, she managed to get a grip on a tangle of broken branches and foliage being carried along by the river and pulled herself on top of it. As the violence of the surging water gradually receded, her body had finally surrendered, and she'd lost consciousness.

When Robyn had eventually come to, she found herself lying partly submerged in the wet mud of the riverbank, the raft of foliage that had saved her life entwined in the trailing branches of a Safsaf willow tree that overhung the river.

Every muscle aching, her leg wound red and throbbing, she had wanted nothing more than to lie there and sleep, but an inbuilt survival instinct, instilled in her from years of living and working in the bushveld, told her that to do so was to invite certain death.

Hauling herself from the clinging mud, she'd been relieved to find that the rugged, waterproof torch she'd been carrying in her trouser pocket for weeks was still working. She found a lonely piece of chocolate too, and remembered Grant giving it to her. How long ago was that? She missed him.

As Robyn played the torch's beam around the water's edge, she saw dozens of sets of animal tracks. This was obviously a popular watering hole for the local wildlife, and none of it needed to be genetically engineered to pose a danger to her.

Finding a well-used path through the foliage, she'd made her way away from the river as quickly as possible. She knew that she needed to find somewhere warm and dry to spend the night, and she needed to find it quickly.

She ended up in a small, safe cave, where she gathered

as much tinder and dry brush wood as she could scavenge, arranging it carefully inside a ring of stones. Then she removed the piece of chocolate from her pocket and unwrapped it. Placing the chocolate to one side she smoothed the foil wrapping flat, then folded and tore it into three long strips, each strip thinner in the middle than at the ends, and placed each one on the floor in front of her.

Making a mental map of where everything was, Robyn turned off the torch. After a few minutes, as her eyes slowly became accustomed to the darkness, she unscrewed the back of the torch and shook one of the lithium batteries into the palm of her hand.

Then came the tricky bit.

Reaching out, she located one of the foil strips, then pressed the wide ends onto the positive and negative terminals of the battery. Immediately the thinner part of the wrapper started to smoulder from the current and there was a flare of light as it ignited.

Robyn thrust the burning wrapper into the tinder, but the flame was already dying and the cave was plunged into blackness once more.

Trying to stay calm, Robyn repeated the procedure with the second strip of foil but, again, the tinder failed to catch. Aware that she only had one piece of foil wrapper remaining, she tried a third time. This time, to her relief, the tinder started to smoulder and crackle and she soon managed to get a respectable fire burning.

As soon as Robyn was satisfied that it wasn't going to go out, she quickly reassembled the torch and checked that it still worked. Then she stripped down to her underwear and draped her wet clothes on rocks around the fire. Feeling warm and dry after what seemed like an eternity, she treated herself to the final square of chocolate. She fell asleep with its sweetness still on her tongue.

Then she'd woken up, coughing. The fire was dead, but her skin was hot and clammy. At once she pictured Tharn: his sweaty, sallow face, his hacking cough that had filled the Land Rover.

'Your friend seems sick,' Niko had said to Rontane. *'Has he been to any urban areas lately?'*

The memory made her moan with fear. 'I'm not sick,' she said out loud, quickly getting dressed. 'I am not sick. *Not sick.'*

Dizzy but determined to prove to herself that she wasn't sick – she couldn't have caught Gerhard's virus – she left the cave and walked as best she could with her bad leg into the beautiful valley, feeling dazed and light-headed. Here she was, face to face with a kind of paradise. *Things are looking up*, she thought. *They've got to be.*

Robyn coughed again. She covered her mouth.

And her palm came away flecked with blood.

The morning sun was creeping above the treetops by the time Ralph woke. He'd slept for far longer than he'd intended. He dressed quickly, grateful that the sun had dried and warmed his mud-stained clothes. Stuffing the foil blanket back into the rucksack, Ralph unwrapped another of the ration packs, eating more slowly this time. From his perch in the tree he could see the terrain around him properly, and it wasn't a pretty sight. Someone had definitely been mining here – for coal, he guessed – and the trees stopped in a line beyond which all plant life had been scoured from the surface. It was small wonder that the flash flood had been so violent, without trees and bushes and roots to slow down the water and hold the soil together.

Finishing the last mouthful of his ration bar Ralph pulled the telescopic sight from the rucksack and began to search for any sign that Robyn might have passed this way. There was none, but a glint of light caught his attention on the far side of the valley. He readjusted the scope and his heart leaped as a cleared area with a collection of buildings swam into focus: he'd found a mine! If it was still in operation then there might be people there, and that could mean access to a radio, food, medical supplies . . . Even if the place had been abandoned, he might still find invaluable equipment there. If Robyn *was* out here, he only hoped that she had spotted the place too.

Stuffing the scope back into the rucksack, Ralph took a moment to fix features on the mountainside that he could use to keep his bearings, then he scrambled down the tree. He set off towards the mine with renewed vigour. The ground beneath his feet was treacherously slippery and littered with razor-sharp rocks. As he edged gingerly around an awkwardly protruding outcrop of rock, Ralph's hand touched something smooth and round. He looked down to see what appeared to be a giant fossilised turtle shell sticking out of the soft mudstone. It was almost five feet across! As he looked around he realised that he could see other fossils, revealed by the landslide.

Raw materials for Gerhard, Ralph thought, *right here on his doorstep.*

Ralph resumed his cautious progress across the field of fossils, feeling unsettlingly like a first-person shooter in one of his games, only unarmed and low on health. He tried to keep out of direct view of anyone who might be watching from the mine, and regularly scanned his surroundings to check that nothing was coming up behind him. There were no save points where he could respawn in real life. If he was caught, it was game over.

The sun was nearly at its zenith by the time Ralph reached the far side of the valley.

His mouth dry from the baking sun, and his fingertips cracked and bleeding from the sharp rocks, Ralph climbed until he had a clear line of sight to the untidy cluster of sheds and prefabricated huts that made up the mine workings. They stood beyond a tall rusty fence crowned with barbed wire. He pulled the telescopic sight from his rucksack and squinted through it, trying to make out any sign of movement inside the buildings, but the entire place was eerily quiet. If there was anyone here, the chances of him scaling the fence without being spotted were virtually non-existent.

Instead, he turned his attention to an open-fronted garage structure on *his* side of the fence where a rust-streaked digger and two battered dump trucks sat covered in a ragged tarpaulin. If he couldn't go *over* the fence, then perhaps he could cut *through* it? And if he was going to find anything to help him with that, then the garage seemed like a logical place to start.

Slipping the scope back into the rucksack Ralph began to skirt around the edge of the mine, keeping low behind the piles of rocks and old mining equipment, until he reached the garage. A long wooden workbench ran along the back wall, but the only tools there were rusted and broken. If he could find a good rock, that might make a hammer for a chisel he'd found, which looked as ancient as the fossils strewn outside. It would be noisy work, though, trying to chip his way through a fence . . .

The sound of something heavy being dragged across the ground made him freeze. Picking up a warped, cobwebbed crowbar from the workbench, Ralph began to creep back towards the garage entrance. The dragging sound was getting closer, and Ralph realised he was trapped in the garage.

Knowing that the element of surprise was the only thing in his favour, Ralph took a deep breath and burst out into the open, wielding the crowbar above his head as if it was a broadsword.

The sight that greeted him stopped him dead in his tracks.

In front of him was another titanoboa, one nearly twice the size of the one he had fought off yesterday.

Not again. Terror froze Ralph where he stood as the titanoboa reared up and leaned its head to one side then the other. Ralph saw the sinister redness of each eye in turn. *God, can I never catch a break?* Adrenaline washed through his body. Every detail of the prehistoric snake looked vivid and sharp. He could see the tiny movements of its breathing, the flicker of each pupil dilating in the dappled light. *Hold still*, Ralph told himself. *Third time is the charm. Maybe this time I'll get past it without –*

With a deafening hiss, the humongous beast surged towards him.

12

Ralph flung the crowbar into the titanoboa's face. It recoiled with an angry snap of its jaws, giving Ralph time to hurl himself past it. He dived away from it, rolled, then used his momentum to spring back to his feet, sprinting away from the garage and the barbed-wire fence towards the trees. He knew they offered a false shelter – one of these giant snakes had attacked him just yesterday in dense bushveld – but as the slithering rush of the giant snake behind him filled his ears, Ralph clung to the thought of getting *away*.

But as he tried to quicken his step, he slipped in the wet mud and fell on his face. The rasping hiss of the titanoboa filled the air. With a moan of terror, Ralph rolled over, staring up in revulsion at the sight he guessed would be his last: the enormous, fanged jaws of the ultimate predator snake closing around him . . .

But the titanoboa had stopped. It swayed from side to side, like it had before.

Part of Ralph's brain was still screaming at him to get up and run, but he was well within striking range of the predasaur and knew that speed couldn't save him. Slowly, cautiously, he pushed himself back through the mud using his heels and elbows. The snake did not react. With small, slow movements, Ralph went on pushing himself back. When the serpent still made no move, he got gingerly to his feet and backed away further.

The titanoboa seemed to lose all interest. It turned away from him, travelling towards the fence, hissing, easily covering thirty metres in one horrible burst of movement.

Ralph took a deep, slow breath. Why hadn't the monster attacked him when he was helpless? *Don't push your luck*, a voice screamed in his head. *Get the hell out of here!* But where was he meant to go? If he was going to find Robyn, he needed supplies and equipment.

And if I'm going to find them anywhere, he thought, *it's in one of those buildings.*

Cautiously, Ralph moved forward – skirting the snake but still heading towards the fence. Immediately, the titanoboa thrust its head towards Ralph, its long, horribly thick tongue flicking in and out. Ralph took a hasty step back again and the snake stopped.

It's reacting, Ralph realised. *My walking towards the fence sets it off, and my retreating calms it down.*

The conclusion was as weird as it was inescapable.

He breathed it aloud. 'This snake monster's been *trained*!'

For a moment he thought of the old snake charmers from India and North Africa, apparently controlling their serpents with a tune they played on their *pungi*. But Ralph couldn't see this brutish monster giving music the time of day; besides, he knew that snakes lacked an outer ear, they 'heard' through vibrations alone.

The titanoboa eyed him balefully, then slithered away as though it had lost interest, following the line of the fence. Ralph watched it go with fearful gratitude. This one wasn't running wild like the one that had attacked their truck. A thought struck him. Had it been trained to patrol the old mine? Perhaps it was rewarded with regular food. The thing must have eaten well recently if it was only concerned with scaring away intruders, not ingesting them.

Was it guarding whatever lay beyond the fence?

What if that 'whatever' was Robyn?

As he backed towards the cover of the trees, Ralph resolved to find another way into whatever was hidden behind the old fence.

Forty kilometres away, through the truck's broken windscreen, Grant stared out at the wild scenery along the mountain road. His body was wedged into the triangle formed by the edge of the seat and the passenger door, and his eyes were beginning to flicker closed. It felt like he, Xai and Niko had been travelling for weeks, dumped by the poachers like trash on the back seat with their hands and ankles tied. Realistically, though, they could only have been in transit for twenty-four hours.

That was more than long enough.

First, Rontane had driven them to her camp, where her poacher gang joined her to rest and regroup. A log fire cracked and sputtered, the body of a wild bush pig turning on an improvised spit above the flames. The aroma made Grant's stomach growl like a cheetah. But there was no meat for them. One of the poachers, a short, stocky man called Chikondi with a mean scowl, dished out *phutu*, a traditional South African porridge made from maize. He slopped ladles of the thick gruel from a large cooking pot onto flat stones that served as basic plates. The *phutu* was thick and burnt. Niko grimaced and turned away.

'We'd better eat,' Grant had told her softly. 'For what's ahead, I reckon we'll need our strength.'

After resting overnight the poachers had cleared their camp, and now travelled in convoy over the veldt and onto a narrow, winding pass. A Land Rover travelled behind the battered truck while a car led the way in front. Grant hoped Roland was OK; it was weird to think the group had lost its leader. From the slump of Xai's shoulders, he was feeling Roland's absence too.

Could I step up to take charge if I needed to? Grant wondered, but reached no conclusions.

He had watched the dawn stir life into the heavy darkness, soothing away the deep bruises of the storm clouds. As the strengthening sun rose over the landscape, the dark basalt peaks of the Lebombo Mountains appeared above the haze-shrouded country, ringing the horizon like distant prison walls. A lush valley bursting with vegetation plunged away from them and the earth steamed, shaking an odour of freshness from the grasses. A golden flock of orioles fled noisily as the truck rumbled past, and cicadas kept up their throaty celebration of the rain passing.

For Grant, concentrating on the wildlife was a way of keeping his brain from picking over their predicament. To have escaped capture for so long, to have triumphed over unnatural predators, to have expended so much nerve and ingenuity – only to fall prey to a sickening lowlife like Kali Rontane! He watched as, one hand on the wheel, the poacher driving them breakfasted on rusks and coffee from a flask. Its thick, bitter smell clashed with the wholesome, post-storm fragrance of the air.

'I know where we're going,' Xai announced suddenly. 'Yonker's place stands on the summit here – Gokomere Lodge.'

'So we're dropping in on the man who helped raze Gauda to the ground,' said Niko bleakly.

'Rontane, are you working with Yonker?' Grant demanded.

'Mbato arranged for pick-up from here,' she said over her shoulder. 'It's a good place to land a helicopter.'

They had reached the end of the road – in more ways than one. Gokomere Lodge was a complex of buildings nestled on a plateau above the N'wanetsi River. The reception building had double-height windows at the front and back of the building, so arriving guests could look straight through to the magnificent scenery beyond. Statues of an elephant and a giraffe flanked the entrance. Through the large windows on the far side of the building Grant glimpsed the azure of swimming pools linked over different levels; the sparkling water reminded him how thirsty he was. Further down the hill were about a dozen smaller buildings, which Grant guessed were guest rooms, each an elegant hybrid of a traditional round hut and a spacious log cabin, each with a wide modern deck facing the river.

The place should have been bustling with staff pampering a small number of exclusive guests, but it was eerily deserted. No trucks or transport sat in the dusty parking bays. Even the day seemed to hold its breath, the beating sun untroubled by even a whisper of a breeze. The magnificent view held Grant entranced for a moment despite his fear, but Xai was looking only at the ground, staring intently all around.

He's a Bakho tracker, Grant realised. *He's reading the land.*

Rontane was taking a less subtle approach. She kicked the door to the reception building. 'Yonker?' she bawled. 'Open up. I've got some gifts here that need wrapping . . .'

There was no reply.

'No one home,' Grant muttered.

'There were many vehicles here,' Xai said. 'They left in a hurry.'

Niko shrugged. 'Maybe they were trying to outrun the virus.'

'Chikondi,' Rontane called to the Land Rover behind them. 'Fetch the battering ram. We'll break in.'

A few seconds passed, then the Land Rover door swung open and Chikondi got out. He staggered to the rear of the Land Rover like he was drunk, but stopped before he got there, leaning against the rear passenger door, panting for breath. Then he coughed, showering the window with specks of blood.

Grant jolted backwards. 'He's got it. Chikondi's got the virus!'

Niko stared at him. 'If Rontane's men have been carrying that virus, any of us could have caught it too!'

13

Robyn walked on through the valley. The light hurt her eyes, and the vivid colours of leaves and flowers seemed to trail through her vision, as if her sight was taking a second to catch up with her.

All seemed still and silent under the cruel glare of the sun. Robyn knew that dangerous game could be closing in all around her. Leopards. Cheetahs. Lions. Black mambas. Or perhaps the titanoboa had scared everything away. Only the shrill call of a bird now and then told her that anything was alive here besides her.

She'd lost track of how long she'd been walking. The coughing fits were growing more frequent. The burning ache of fatigue branded her muscles. The cut on her leg was red and inflamed. She'd even started hearing things – strange bird calls and the buzz of a helicopter. She'd hidden, but seen no trace of movement in the sky. Maybe her infected leg was giving her this fever?

Maybe it was more than that.

Robyn staggered on. She had to find Ralph. Or find

someone to help her look for him. However sick she felt, she couldn't fail her brother. Together they might stand a chance of finding Dad and Xai and the others. On her own . . .

Then she stumbled and fell, landing in a stream. The shock of the cold water brought Robyn to her senses. She sipped from it; it tasted sour and earthy from the debris washed down with the flood, and she spat it back out. She was so thirsty, so hungry, felt so goddamn terrible.

With leaden limbs, Robyn got up and made for the shade of a wall of rock. Trees and shrubs clung to the steep slope, sheltering against the rock face. But as she got closer, she blinked: what had looked to her like a seam in the rock face was actually two overlapping sections of cliff face. As Robyn stepped up to the gap, she saw that it led to a narrow passage that snaked sideways into the cliff before opening into a larger cave.

As if in a dream, Robyn went inside. There the air was cool, and she smelled an earthy dampness as a faint breeze blew from the deeper darkness. It was a relief after the heat and noise of the bushveld outside. She coughed again, the hacking sound echoing back to her as she made her way along the tunnel. And when she reached its end, Robyn gasped.

She was in a natural stronghold deep inside the mountain: a gaping cavern with about a third at one end open to the sky. Sunlight streamed in, lighting up plants, a crystal-clear lake of water to one side, and even a cluster of large trees stretching up to the sun. Higher peaks to one side and tall trees like sentries across the opening helped to screen the cavern from outside eyes.

It was a hidden jewel, deep inside the mountains.

A pit cave, she realised. *But I've come in from the mountainside instead of down from above.*

The water looked so beautiful and inviting. Robyn felt like she was baking from the inside. She stumbled unsteadily down the slope.

And then a figure stepped from behind a boulder in front of her.

It was a young woman in a brightly patterned slip. Her skin was etched with tribal marks, striping down her cheeks. Xai had similar marks on his face and chest, each signifying a pivotal moment in his childhood journey, and Robyn realised this woman must belong to the Bakho. She thought for a moment that she was dreaming; surely the land-grabbers and the illegal mine owners had driven the indigenous tribes away from here?

But the woman didn't shimmer and disappear. She took a step towards Robyn, her face grave, her eyes dark and piercing.

'Please,' Robyn said, coughing again. 'Don't come any closer. I'm sick. I might give the sickness to you . . .'

The woman kept coming. She spoke in a language that Robyn couldn't understand, but the clicks she made told Robyn that it was a Khoisan dialect, spoken by the first inhabitants of southern Africa. She heard movement behind her and turned – to find three tribesmen with lethal-looking spears blocking her way.

'Don't you understand? I'm sick. Really sick!' Robyn covered her mouth as she turned to them, trying to make her eyes focus. But the men remained shadows haunting her sight until her eyelids closed, and her knees buckled, and she fell to the damp earth. She felt like she had fallen under a magnifying lens, concentrating the sun's rays. She was burning up.

As the heat and the darkness overwhelmed her, Robyn dreamed that she might reach the soothing water in this strange paradise. The last thing she heard was the sound of the tribespeople moving closer.

Grant sat in the cool of a downstairs guest room, hugging his knees. His wrists throbbed from the tightness of the zip-tie cuffs, but it was the feeling of dread in his stomach that was hardest to bear.

Because on the other side of the room, slumped on the unmade bed, moaning and drifting in and out of consciousness, was Chikondi.

'He's meant to be watching us,' Grant muttered. 'Instead, we're watching him.'

'If only they hadn't nailed shut the window from the outside,' Xai said.

'So we could open it for ventilation?' said Niko.

Xai shook his head. 'So we could get the hell out of here, find Roland and make a break.'

'Pretty sure that's why they nailed it.' Grant leaned his head back against the wall. 'Where's Yonker, do you think? Did I hear him say something on the radio about bailing cos of family?'

'That's right,' Xai agreed. 'Roland and I heard him say his guests were clearing out as the country's lockdown kicked in.'

'You'd think this place would be perfect for sitting out a pandemic,' said Grant. 'But I guess if he had family elsewhere who got sick . . .'

'I didn't think Yonker had any family,' said Xai quietly.

Then Niko banged on the door, drowning him out. 'For God's sake!' she shouted. 'Chikondi needs medical help!'

'Then it's a good job you're a doctor, isn't it?' Rontane's voice made Grant jump, as a key turned in the door lock. 'I've found a first aid kit. Move away from the door, or you'll be the one who needs it.'

Grant snorted. 'You think sticking a band-aid on your friend is gonna help?'

Xai shook his head, advising Grant to save his breath, and shifted away from the door, giving Chikondi a wide berth. Rontane pushed inside with a large cool box in one hand and a handgun in the other. She still wore her shades, with a neckerchief tied over her mouth and nose.

She pointed to Chikondi. 'He's got your virus, hasn't he?'

'It's *not* ours,' Niko insisted. 'It could be many things. Lassa fever, for instance.'

'You get that from rats, don't you?' said Grant and he turned to sneer at Rontane. 'Hanging around with you, sounds likely.'

She kicked him, her boot's steel-capped toe making him wince, then handed the box to Niko. 'All right, doc. Make him more comfortable.'

Niko glared up at her. 'What's in it for us?'

110

'I know you doctor types. All life's precious, right? Even his.' She smiled smugly. 'And if you don't, I'll go give your boyfriend some more cuts and bruises to go with his cuts and bruises.'

Grant saw the hope jump into Niko's eyes at the mention of Roland. 'He's all right?'

'For now,' said Rontane.

'What about Ralph and Robyn?' Grant said. 'Where are they?'

But Rontane just strode from the room, slamming the door behind her. A key turned in the lock.

'Something must have happened,' Xai muttered.

'Maybe Ralph and Robyn got away?' said Grant. 'You think the snake . . .'

'Don't focus on things we can't know,' Xai told him firmly. 'It's the possibilities here and now that count if we're to get out of this.'

Niko lifted the lid on the cool box. 'This is well equipped,' she remarked, and pulled out some surgical masks.

'Yonker was always a good field medic,' Xai said.

Niko passed masks to Xai and Grant before affixing her own, the usually simple act complicated by the wrist restraints.

'We just have to hope that we haven't been exposed already. If you'll help me, Grant, I'll give Chikondi a shot of ribavirin – it's an antiviral drug.' Niko pulled a syringe from the cool box. 'If he responds to the shot, he's got Lassa fever. If he hasn't, he has the predasaur virus – and it will kill him.'

111

14

Ralph was moving as quickly as he could through the girdle of land surrounding the mine workings, making sure to keep a safe distance from the fence. He figured that some sort of technology must be employed to 'trigger' the titanoboa – motion sensors, or perhaps pressure sensors buried just beneath the ground. If there was a chain of such sensors, they could transmit a vibration for the giant snake to follow, leading it to the scene of an attempted break-in.

That's what I'd do, Ralph thought. *Question is, how do I beat it?* He was looking for a quick way in – some breach in the fence that might allow swift access before the serpent could reach the scene. Then there would be a barbed-wire fence between the two of them and he could make his way into the territory beyond. Finally, Ralph came across a baobab tree leaning drunkenly towards the fence. The soil around it had washed away, either in a flood or from mining activity. Its stubby, twisted limbs, reaching for the sky from its broad trunk, looked more like roots than branches; small wonder it was known as the upside-down tree. Right now, Ralph figured it could make a useful ladder, enabling him to swing over the barbed wire crowning the fence.

Stealthily, he ran over to the tree, aware that his movements might be sending invisible signals to the titanoboa – *I'm here! Catch me if you can!* Ralph scrambled up the broad trunk and threw himself into the branches, clambering through their tangling embrace. From here he could see a large concrete platform marked with lights around its perimeter. A *helipad*, he realised, and remembered the helicopter he'd heard. Were they operating out of here? That would bode well for finding supplies – but it would increase the likelihood of finding trouble too.

Whatever. If he could just find a dirt bike so he could cover the terrain faster, or a four-by-four – something that might afford him a little protection from game and monsters – then he'd stand a much better chance of finding Robyn.

Once he was clear of the fence he dropped down from the tree, his ankles jarring despite the soft mud that had broken his fall. His elation at getting over the fence was met by the realisation that climbing out again was going to be a hell of a lot harder. But with luck he would find equipment somewhere – cutting equipment, perhaps, that would allow him out with whatever spoils he could find.

No one had come running at the sound of him landing. The compound seemed just as deserted on this side of the fence as it was out there in the wilderness.

Cautiously, looking all around, Ralph made for the nearest garage and prayed his luck would hold.

The guest room in Gokomere Lodge was becoming stuffy and warm. Grant distracted himself by staring out of the window at the magnificent view down to the N'wanetsi River. Slow hours had been punctuated all too regularly by Chikondi's hacking cough. Niko was bent over the sofa where the sick poacher lay, frowning above her mask, blotting the sweat from his face with a folded cloth. As for Xai, he was still sitting on the floor by the door, seemingly immune to the stress of time passing. Grant supposed that his soldier days had prepared him for long periods of confinement.

'I'd have thought that a helicopter would be here for us by now,' Niko said. 'Given how hard Mbato's been on our backs.'

'We blew up the last one,' Grant reminded her. 'Besides, Mbato can't admit to paying poachers to catch us. Picking us up, taking us back . . . I guess it has to be done by the book.'

Chikondi groaned, a long and painful noise.

'There's nothing I can do,' Niko said hoarsely, turning away. 'He's not responding to treatment – because there isn't any. He's got the virus, I'm certain.'

Grant felt a chill, despite the stuffy heat. 'I hope these masks work. If they don't –'

They all jumped as something clanged against the windowpane.

'What the hell was that?' Grant hissed, gazing out. There was no sign of life through the glass. 'Maybe a bird flew into the window?'

As he looked down, he frowned. The long nails hammered into the window frame to stop it opening had been removed. 'When did that happen?' he whispered, trying the window. It opened a crack.

Niko gasped. 'How did you do that?'

Xai quickly got up and joined Grant. 'Someone must have done it from the outside.'

'But I've been standing here,' Grant said. 'Didn't see anything.'

'Perhaps the bang on the window was to get your attention,' Xai said. 'Maybe not all the guests left after all!'

Grant started to push the window open a little more, then he heard the dull buzz of a helicopter approaching. 'Oh, no,' he whispered. 'I guess that's not a late holiday booking.'

The door was kicked open. Rontane swaggered in, a revolver in each hand. The mask over her mouth couldn't disguise her sneer. 'Time to go.'

'You can't hand us over without taking precautions,' Niko said. 'We may be infectious. We could give those soldiers the virus and they could spread it –'

'Let them,' said Rontane, gesturing for them to move towards the door. 'As long as I get my money.'

Grant stabbed a finger at Chikondi. 'Your friend is going to die!'

'So? Everybody dies,' Rontane said coldly.

Another of Rontane's men ran in, a rangy character in a red tracksuit top and khaki shorts. 'He's gone,' the man said. 'Ballantyne's gone!'

Niko actually gasped out loud. 'What?'

Rontane rounded on her pet thug, jabbing a revolver in his face. 'How the hell can he be gone, Femi? He was tied up in a room with the window nailed shut from the outside!'

Excitement stirring his insides, Grant thought of the way their own window had been freed. That had come too late to help them, but if Roland had got out . . . perhaps there was a chance for them all?

Rontane turned on Xai. 'What do you know of this?'

'Nothing,' he said calmly.

'How about you?' Femi thrust his gun into Grant's face.

Grant did his best not to show he was intimidated. 'You saw Niko's reaction. She couldn't fake that.'

'And you know we were locked in this room,' said Niko. 'How could we know anything?'

'We'll find Ballantyne,' Femi growled. 'We'll take this whole place apart.'

'In front of Mbato's men, you idiot?' Rontane hissed. 'I should maybe invite them in to wait, make them a cup of rooibos, huh?' She grabbed Niko by the hair. 'If we threaten this one, Ballantyne will have to surrender.'

Niko gasped as she was dragged out of the room. Femi pushed Xai outside and motioned with the gun for Grant to follow. Hands raised, he obeyed. More poachers were waiting outside, automatic weapons held ready. Through the full-height glass walls of the reception lounge, Grant could see the helicopter growing larger in the pale blue sky, a giant mosquito zeroing in on its prey. How many soldiers were on board? The stakes were high – life or death – and Grant knew he had to be ready.

Rontane kicked the back of Niko's calves so she fell to her knees on the patio outside. Another poacher came out and gripped Niko by the back of the neck, leaving Rontane free to stalk about. 'Ballantyne!' she bellowed over the rush of rotors. 'Come out now or I blow off your lady-love's kneecaps.'

Grant clenched his fists. The trees began to blow as the helicopter readied itself to land.

'I mean it!' Rontane shouted. 'I get as much for her in pieces as I do for her intact. You like her cos she's pretty, right? Give it up, or she won't stay pretty for long.'

The copter swung in towards the landing spot. As it turned, Grant saw that its door was open, revealing black-uniformed figures with rifles at the ready. Rontane turned angrily and held up a hand to Femi, warning him to stay back. At the same time, the rest of her men gathered in a loose group at the edge of the open area outside the building, weapons raised, looking around for Roland.

The copter landed. Soldiers spewed out. Grant held his breath, felt the sweat trickle down his back. Then gunfire raked the helicopter, sending sparks shooting from its armoured carapace. Someone had opened fire! The cockpit windscreen bloomed with little white scars as bullets ground at the glass.

'No!' Rontane shouted. But any other protests were cut off as the soldiers returned fire. Two of the poachers were cut down, dancing in the chatter of bullets. Niko's captor was hit and fell backwards. Niko threw herself forward, flat down on the patio. At the same time, Rontane turned and sprinted for the reception area. The full-length windows shattered under the onslaught of bullets before the Queen of the Poachers could reach shelter, and she fell in a hail of broken glass. More poachers with guns appeared, firing wildly, driving the soldiers back into defensive positions around the helipad.

At the same time, Xai raised his arms as if in surrender. But then he placed his palms together and swept his arms downward hard, in a cutting motion. As his hands came level with his stomach, he opened out his elbows and the cable ties snapped under the dynamic force. The next moment, Xai had snatched the gun from Femi's hand and shoved him hard, propelling him into the flying glass.

'Down, Grant!' Xai yelled.

As the rattle of guns went on tearing at the silence, Grant had already flung himself down behind a heavy oak coffee table. He watched in horror as Femi turned even as he fell, revealing a vicious knife in his hand. He hurled it, and it struck Xai's gun arm. Xai grunted as the blade bit deep; he lost his grip on the gun as he staggered back, hiding behind the statue of the elephant. One tusk was blown into fragments by a stray bullet.

Wild-eyed, Femi was about to get up and retrieve his weapon. But Grant shoved the coffee table across the wooden floor into Femi's legs, and the poacher sprawled to the floor.

Before Grant could get up to join Xai, a soldier in a

ballistic face mask ran into the room, holding Niko in front of him like a human shield. The soldier's gun swung down.

Grant found himself staring down the barrel.

15

'Grant, move!' The soldier tore off his face mask – to reveal the battered features of Roland Ballantyne. Grant realised numbly that Niko wasn't being used as a human shield. Roland was shielding her with *his* body.

As more bullets sprayed the reception area, Xai ducked out from behind the statue to return fire, the machine gun back in his bloody hands, the knife still embedded in his arm. Grant scrambled to hunker down behind him, and Roland half-carried Niko there.

'What happened?' Grant demanded. 'Why'd the poachers open fire on the helicopter?'

'They didn't. I did,' Roland panted. 'Made the Recces think the poachers were firing on them, so they'd fire back. Might even the odds a little for us.'

'Bold thinking.' Xai jerked his head back towards the room where they'd been held with Chikondi. 'Now, fall back. We can get out through the window there. I'll cover you.'

Roland clapped a hand on Xai's shoulder and removed the knife. 'Go to it, little rogue.'

Xai let off a stream of gunfire through the broken windows as Grant raced to the bedroom. Roland followed with Niko.

She hugged him. 'Who helped you get out?'

'I don't know.' Roland used the knife he'd pulled from Xai's shoulder to saw through the plastic cuffs on Grant's wrists. 'But I found this uniform and the gun stowed beneath the opened window. They must belong to Yonker.'

A blood-curdling scream came from outside.

Roland pointed to the window. 'Shift!'

Grant climbed out and dropped to the ground. He could hear shouting and gunfire. Seconds later, Xai had dropped down beside him. Roland lowered Niko out through the window and Grant helped her down.

There was a crash from inside as the door to the room was kicked open. Roland jumped down.

'Rontane?' Chikondi's hoarse, delirious shout came from inside the room. 'What's happening?'

A single gunshot was his answer. Then he was silent.

'Stay close,' Roland hissed to his group. They set off across the manicured lawn, Roland swinging the rifle from side to side to cover the deck and the land sloping down towards the river. Grant and Niko followed, while Xai took up the rear. Grant risked a look behind and saw a shadow appear at the open window. Xai fired and the soldier fell back.

'Come on!' Grant ran with Niko to where Roland was sheltering at the corner of the building.

A man's voice rang out from behind nearby thorn trees. 'Mbato must be trying to take the prisoners without paying. Kill them on sight.'

'Dammit,' Roland muttered.

Even as he spoke, bullets struck the wall beside Grant. He dived for cover. Roland swung around and fired three shots into the bushes while Xai grabbed Niko's arm and charged away with her for the cover of nearby trees.

'With me, Grant!' Roland shouted as he darted away, firing again, this time at two poachers who'd appeared from behind one of the guest villas.

One of them hurled something before they dropped.

Grant swore as a rusty metal pineapple landed in the neat grass ahead of him. 'Grenade!' he yelled.

On instinct, he darted wildly to his left. Too late, he realised that Roland was racing to the right, trailing Xai and Niko for the cover of a low boundary wall. Grant skidded to a stop, about to change direction. Time seemed to slow. How many seconds left until the grenade blew? Grant started to run again, away from the others. He dived over a large ornamental bush in the lawn.

He was still in mid-air when the grenade exploded.

Ralph was trying to stay positive, but there seemed to be nothing here that might help him find Robyn: no tools, no supplies, no vehicles. And definitely no signs that his sister had been here. The buildings he'd investigated so far had been empty save for the lingering stink of musk and filth. Animals had been kept here at some point. From the scratches and claw marks in the concrete, they had been wild animals.

This place might have been a mine once, but someone

had clearly repurposed it. All those fossils . . . Could this be where Gerhard had started his predasaur research?

In one building, half the wall had been clawed away, and the twisted metal remains of cages were testament to the strength of the beasts they must once have contained. In another, Ralph found a pile of weathered shovels and an ominous carpet of bleached bones and skulls; from the looks of them, they had belonged to herbivores like impala or wildebeest. Many of the bones had been snapped in two.

What happened here? he thought grimly. *What is that titanoboa still protecting?*

Ralph carried the sturdiest shovel with him as he followed rusted railway tracks through the silent yard. His mouth was dry and his limbs ached, but he kept going. The battered mine cars that once had carried ore from the main works stood abandoned in the sidings. No birds called out overhead. Even the cicadas had stopped singing. Water from the flood lay pooled in hollows, perfect silvered mirrors to the late day's sky and lengthening shadows. It was as if nature didn't know what to do here, and had either fled or frozen.

Then Ralph froze too. He wiped his eyes. 'What the hell?'

The rails didn't lead to the mouth of a tunnel or a storage depot, as Ralph had expected. The rocky soil bled into black tarmac and the tracks came to an end on a stretch of modern street. Ralph found himself gazing up at a red-brick hotel with an office block beside it. Tall, ornate streetlamps stood either side of the street like sentries. Across the street stood a florist, a pawn shop and a comic-book store. It was as if a piece of a city had just fallen from the sky. The road ran on to a T junction with a beachfront beyond, complete with funfair. A big wheel and a carousel turned in eerie silence. There was no sign of anyone.

Am I hallucinating or something? Frowning, Ralph stooped and picked up a rock from the ground. Then he tossed it at the beachfront. The stone bounced in mid-air and fell to the ground.

'It's not real,' he muttered. The view ahead of him looked like a generated 3D image. *Like something out of a video game*, Ralph realised. *This has got Gerhard's fingerprints all over it.* He tossed a stone up in front of one of the streetlamps and watched its shadow swoop across the beachfront like a meteor. Yes, the streetlamps must be sophisticated projectors.

Suddenly he heard the pounding of heavy footsteps, enough to shake the ground. A woolly mammoth charged out from the projected background, the mismatch of scale making it seem even more enormous. Its tusks were bloody and puncture wounds stained its shaggy hide. It stared at Ralph with bloodshot red eyes, trunk curling, afraid and in shock. Then its mouth opened and it trumpeted defiantly. Ralph staggered backwards, realising it meant to charge at him.

Then two more creatures coiled out from whatever space lay hidden behind the backdrop. Jet-black titanoboas, way smaller than the ones he'd met but still twice as long as he was, their meaty tongues flicking out between ivory fangs.

A shadow fell over Ralph. Two camera drones had

appeared, circling like birds of prey. Taking up position to capture the action about to unfold.

Ralph turned to run, but knew it was too late. The mammoth was already lumbering towards him, the snakes flanking it.

There was nowhere to hide.

16

As the grenade detonated, the paradise of Gokomere Lodge disintegrated into hell – and Grant was almost taken along for the ride. The blast carried him through the air, deafened him, and punched the breath from his lungs. He found himself on his back in mud, staring up at a cloud of blue-black smoke, his ears ringing. His legs felt burning hot. He looked down and saw little welts and burns patterning his legs up to his thighs. He gritted his teeth against the pain. Where were the others? He glimpsed movement through the smoke. Was that Roland racing to reach him – or someone else?

Desperate but determined, Grant scrambled up and began a limping zigzag through a complex of guest chalets. He caught a whiff of chlorine and saw that beyond them stood an enormous gymnasium beside the outdoor pools he'd seen earlier. There was a smaller building too, which he guessed must be a pump house, keeping the water clean. The gym must allow guests to work out with the most incredible panoramic views, Grant supposed, but more importantly to him, it meant the hope of changing rooms and lockers. Perhaps he could find a hiding place? In any case, he had no time to think; he had to *run*.

And he did run, straight into a black ops soldier coming the other way from behind the gym building.

Grant froze as the man towered over him. He was about to dive through the man's legs, try to push him off balance, when a small stone flew through the air. It struck the soldier on the temple, and he collapsed.

Grant stared. There, at the far corner of the gym building, stood a girl a few years younger than he was, wearing khakis and a plain shirt. Her cheeks were covered with tribal markings and she wore her hair close-cropped and tightly curled. Grant saw the dark Y of a catapult in one hand; that explained how she'd brought down the unsuspecting soldier.

'Hurry,' she hissed and beckoned him sharply.

With no other options available, Grant ran after her.

In the make-believe street that stood in the middle of the mineworks, Ralph ran for one of the old mine cars. It was too far away, and would offer little cover, but there was nothing else to try.

The mammoth increased its speed as the serpents came closer. The camera drones bobbed down for a closer look, as if sensing that the kill was close. Ralph pushed himself harder but then was nearly thrown off his feet by the shockwaves from a crashing impact behind him. The mammoth bellowed in rage and pain.

Ralph risked a look over his shoulder, and saw that the

mammoth was on the ground. The huge black serpents were writhing and undulating around its legs, holding it fast, crushing it. The attacking titanoboas hooked their hefty fangs into the mammoth's neck, piercing its hairy flesh. Ralph turned away, revolted.

'And CUT!' came a high, nasal voice that turned Ralph's stomach to ice. He looked further down the fake street.

Josef Gerhard stepped into view through the projected backdrop, a sleek tablet in his hand and two armed guards behind him.

'You,' Ralph breathed, clenching his fists. He'd known that Gerhard was behind all this, but it was still a shock to be back face to face with him. 'What is all this?'

'It's my very important research and development tech centre.' Gerhard smiled. 'I'm actually as surprised to see you as you must be to see me. Mbato and I have spent so long trying to track down your little tribe, and here you are, right under my nose. Any more of you here?'

'No,' Ralph said. 'But if you find them, tell them I said hi.'

Gerhard's grin was gloating as he took in Ralph's grubby, bruised appearance. 'You have been in the wars, haven't you? Still. You can relax now. Nowhere left to run.' He nodded back towards the make-believe street. 'Perhaps you'd care to progress a little further through one of my games?'

'No, thanks,' said Ralph. 'So what is this place? Thought you looked after the predasaurs in your private park.'

'That is so. But they were created here.' He bestowed a smile on the two technicians. 'I insist on visiting here by helicopter when my team tell me they've made vital breakthroughs.'

Ralph gestured to the fake street. 'Breakthroughs in making your video game cut-scenes even sicker?'

'Setting up a scene and relying on a predasaur's savagery to carry the action can be hit or miss.' Gerhard flicked his fingers across the surface of the tablet. 'The breakthrough here is one of *control*.' The titanoboas paused, then squirmed away from the miserable corpse of the mammoth. They circled Ralph, eyeing him spitefully.

'I direct everything, Ralph.' Gerhard's bulging eyes didn't blink. 'Everything.'

Ralph couldn't hide his horror. This was far beyond how Gerhard had controlled the cave hyenas that had hunted them in his secret killing grounds. There he'd used drones that could spray scents to attract, or deliver electric shocks to repel. The way he controlled these titanoboas was precise and terrifying.

'Stimulating certain muscles helps human beings to walk again after a spinal injury,' Gerhard went on. 'It's a similar principle. Subjects react automatically within a set of allowed actions. They have no choice.'

'I guess something that slithers on its belly is easier to control than something with four legs,' said Ralph, desperate to keep Gerhard talking while he tried to think of an escape plan. 'But isn't a giant guard snake going to draw attention to this place? Word spreads. You'll have a bunch of hunters on your doorstep.'

'I trust that will be the case. And my drones will be

ready to film their deaths,' said Gerhard calmly. 'Their last moments – suitably enhanced – will contribute to the next and biggest ever version of *Predasaur*. I'm calling it *The Serpent's Lair*.' He opened his arms, as if expecting rapturous applause.

Ralph just stood and stared. 'I didn't see cameras when your snake attacked the poachers.'

'Some of my earliest creations escaped into the wild before full control could be established.' Gerhard gave a mirthless smile, and Ralph felt a pang of fear. How many more were out in the wild – perhaps even now stalking his injured sister?

'Today, these beasts are entirely under my command. *The Serpent's Lair* has lifelike graphics, even grislier action – and a wonderful storyline, about a family of dangerous ecoterrorists who are consumed by their own genetic creations . . .'

Ralph narrowed his eyes. 'So, you've already tricked the real world into believing we're the bad guys, and now you're basing your whole game around it. Even though *you're* the one who let the virus loose!' He glanced nervously at the titanoboas. 'Is it all predasaurs that carry it? No, can't be. You'd all be infected by now.'

'Stefan was the only member of staff affected,' Gerhard revealed. 'The fool got himself bitten handling a specimen of *Desmodus draculae* – a type of vampire bat resurrected from the early Holocene period. I had the work incinerated – or rather, your father did. Right?' Gerhard winked and wagged a finger. 'I'm the one who'll clean up after your terrible, destructive mistakes. And *you* are going to help me.'

'You can go to –'

'I know where your sister is.'

Everything stopped for Ralph.

'Robyn is alive. And if you behave yourself, you might just see her again.' Gerhard smirked. 'If you *really* behave yourself, you might even see her alive.'

Ralph stared at him, trying to control his breathing as the titanoboas slithered closer and their hissing grew louder in his ears. *Rob's alive*, he thought, *and Gerhard's my only chance of finding her*.

Slowly, he raised his hands in surrender. The snakes stared at him stonily, eyes narrowed, tongues flickering.

As if tiring of his audience, Gerhard turned away, tapping at his tablet. The titanoboas reared up and edged closer. Ralph recoiled and moved away a few metres. One of the serpentine monsters moved around to his right, and he retreated further.

They're herding me, he realised with a chill. *But where to?*

17

At Gokomere Lodge, Grant, too, had no idea where he was being taken. The girl with the catapult led him around the back of the gymnasium to where the pool stretched out towards a flight of stone steps. The steps led down to a smaller infinity pool surrounded by bamboo sun loungers on a raised deck where guests could rest gazing out towards herds of animals drinking from the river far below, away from the carnage here. The girl led Grant not onto the raised deck but beneath it. Then she thumped her shoulder against the timber panelling beside the pool wall, and a section swung inwards on concealed hinges.

'Secret hiding place?' Grant whispered.

'Storage. Pool chemicals,' the girl informed him. She ducked into the narrow, shadowed space beyond and Grant squeezed in behind her. The sharp reek of disinfectant was almost overpowering, but for the first time in forever he felt safe. Water gurgled above and around them as the pumps kept the water circulating from the overflow. The noise would help hide them too.

'Thank you,' Grant panted as the girl quickly pushed the wooden panel closed again. 'Who are you?'

'Moth,' the girl said. 'My name is Moth.'

'What are you doing here? Where did you –'

'Be quiet, please.' There were tiny gaps between the wooden planks, and she knelt on the dusty ground to put her eye to them.

Grant copied her. His view was severely restricted, but he glimpsed figures running and heard gunfire. Someone shouted, 'This way!'

'I need to find my friends,' Grant muttered. He placed a hand on the hinged panel.

Moth noticed the movement and snatched his arm. 'No.'

'You don't get it. I need to at least try.' Grant swallowed hard. 'A couple of weeks ago, I didn't go after this boy, Luke, and . . . he died. Alone.' Images of the lanky boy, screaming as he ran across the rocks, terrified, burned through Grant's brain and he got back to his feet. 'I can't let that happen to anyone else –'

'You've got no weapons.'

Grant nodded to the handmade catapult she clutched. 'What about your catty? You brought down that soldier with a single rock.'

'That was a lucky shot. You've got rocks *in* your head if you think we can bring down everyone. I know the land here – I was trying to get you guys away.' She looked at him, watching carefully while he got his emotions under control again. 'I can help you guys. It was me who took the nails out of the window, Grant.'

'You know my name?'

'Heard you, didn't I? Standing at the window. Not noticing me.' She smiled slyly. 'Nobody ever notices Moth.'

'You were hiding here too . . .' Grant considered the tribal markings on the girl's cheeks: she looked like she belonged to an indigenous tribe. 'Moth. Are you from one of the local San communities? Is Moth short for Motholeli?'

'Yes!' She smiled, dark eyes glittering in the lantern light. 'How would you know?'

'My dad leads the Green Freedom Party. He's been trying to get land back for the San. And my friends and I, we've been looking for you, for help –'

'Your friend Xai is of the local people, the Bakho,' Moth broke in. 'He doesn't know the place of hiding?'

'No. It's kind of been a while for him . . .' Grant flinched as gunshots rang out, again and again.

Moth turned quickly back to the tiny cracks in the planks, alert and frowning. Heavy footsteps tapped overhead. Recces or poachers, it was impossible to tell.

'Pray they don't find *our* place of hiding,' Moth said.

Robyn woke in darkness. She breathed in cool, slightly damp air. For a moment she thought she was back in the cave she'd found after the flood, that she'd dreamed her stumbling ordeal through the post-flood landscape. But no, she was lying on something softer. Her fingers strayed to her side and found cotton sheets, stretched over a stiff-sprung mattress. She heard the gentle hum and rush of machines. Was *this* the dream? She prayed not: her throat was sore and her head ached, but she felt stronger than she had in ages. Even her leg no longer hurt.

Robyn opened her eyes and raised her head. A motion sensor registered the movement and her surroundings showed in soft topaz light.

She was in a hospital bed in a large cave filled with modern medical equipment. The floor was smooth poured concrete, but the walls were dark rock. Electrical cables snaked along the floor from outside the door to the medical monitors and other equipment on one side of the chamber.

She felt a tremor of fear. *Gerhard*, she thought. *He must've found me. Picked me up. Taken me . . . Taken me where? Where's Ralph and Dad? Everyone . . .*

Robyn saw that her shoes were at the foot of the bed. She got out of bed, slipped them on and peeled off the sticky patches holding medical sensors against her skin. The world spun in a whirl of nausea but she closed her eyes and breathed deeply and it passed. Then, carefully, she stepped out from the cave into a rough-hewn corridor.

There were patterns on the walls, ancient rusty inks and etchings showing spindly human figures dancing around oversized buffalo and wildebeest. One group held what looked like spears to ward off a pack of hyenas.

Been there, done that, thought Robyn with a shudder. She assumed the drawings depicted the Bakho. Her eyes lingered on one of the human figures, which had been drawn larger than the rest – seen from the side, lying on his back, he wore a headdress, and one arm was raised in the air as if pointing to heaven.

A sangoma, Robyn realised; a shaman, or witch doctor, as they used to be called. When she'd been small, Xai used to tell her and Ralph tales of the sangoma he'd known as a child, back when he still lived with the tribe. They would ingest poison to receive visions: truths to guide his people.

The sangoma taught us that pain makes us strong, Xai had told them. *That suffering can bring wisdom if you look in the right way.*

'I should be the strongest, smartest person around in that case,' Robyn muttered, pressing on through the gloomy tunnel.

At the turning, she saw someone ahead of her and froze. It was a young woman, wearing bright prints. The woman spoke in Bakho – Robyn couldn't understand the words, but she understood the urgency on the young woman's face.

'I know you,' Robyn said quietly. 'I saw you . . . when I had the fever . . .'

The woman started towards Robyn. Alarmed, Robyn turned and retraced her steps. But her way was blocked by another figure: a bear of a man with an intricate pattern of scars beaded under his eyes and across his cheekbones. He wore a patchwork outfit, a white tunic and kilt overlaid with scraps of colourful geometric prints, cheetah fur and leather. His arms were tied with feathers and tufts from the manes of lions.

Robyn held her ground, staring up at him. 'You're a sangoma,' she whispered. It was as if, by simply thinking of them, she had conjured one in this weird underground place.

The sangoma gazed down at Robyn. Then a brilliant smile spread over his face. 'You're up and around!' he said in perfect English. 'You know, you had us all very worried here in the settlement.'

'A Bakho settlement?' Robyn felt a spark of hope.

'Correct,' the sangoma said. 'And you may call me Senosi. We have a lot of questions for you.'

'Snap,' Robyn said, suddenly suspicious again. 'Like, how do you know my name?'

'Ah.' The sangoma smiled. 'It was given to me by our other unexpected visitor.'

'What?' Robyn's heart seemed to freeze as her brain processed Senosi's words. 'Who . . .'

'Hey, Rob,' came a voice behind her.

Robyn swung around to see a lanky blond boy standing next to the young woman. His arm was in a sling and his face scarred and swollen, but she recognised him immediately. She just didn't believe what she was seeing.

'Luke!' she breathed.

18

'It's you.' Robyn stared at him in utter disbelief. 'Luke van Rok!'

'Well, what's left of me,' Luke said. Then he smiled, and Robyn ran to him, and seized him in a hug.

'Ouch! Careful, I'm a mess . . .'

'Oh, God, so am I.' Robyn laughed through her tears, sniffing. She'd been so certain that Luke had been slaughtered by the cave hyenas Gerhard had sent after them. They'd all heard his screams. How could he be alive? How could he be *here*? 'I don't believe it. We were sure you had to be dead.'

'Those hyena things tore into me like cheap dog meat,' Luke said. 'I've never known so much pain. I . . .' He stared at her. 'I should never have run like that. Shouldn't have tried to bargain with Gerhard, but . . .'

'You were scared,' Robyn said. 'I get it.' She felt dizzy. 'Luke . . .'

'Easy, now.' Luke pulled awkwardly away from her but kept a hand on her hip to steady her. 'You've been real sick. They said you had the virus.'

'But I can't have,' Robyn argued. 'I'm still here.'

'It is a truly remarkable story,' said Senosi. 'And I will tell it to you once you rest. There will be time to talk with your friend soon.'

Luke nodded. 'Senosi's been really good to me – the whole tribe have.' He gave her a hopeful smile. 'We're safe here.'

'But I've got to find Ralph. Grant, Dad, and . . .' Again, she felt dizzy. 'My head feels so weird.'

'You've been through a lot,' said Senosi. He spoke to the young tribeswoman in Bakho, and she nodded, taking Robyn by the arm. 'You must rest now.'

Luke tried to take Robyn's other arm but Senosi shook his head. 'You must rest too, young man.'

'Aw, c'mon,' Luke protested. 'I've been resting for weeks . . .'

'Your wounds were badly infected. You've made great improvement but you still need rest, just as she does.' Senosi smiled, but his manner was firm. 'Please return to your bed.'

'I have to find Ralph. I can't stay,' Robyn said weakly. 'He's out there, and my dad and Grant and Niko and Xai, they were taken by poachers . . .' She leaned against the wall, shivering. 'I *can't* stay.'

'I think you'll find you can do little else,' Senosi said softly. 'Don't worry. My people know these lands as well as you know your own home. If a stranger walks here, they will find him.' Again, he spoke in his native tongue, and the Bakho woman helped steer Robyn back to her room.

At the turn in the corridor, Robyn glanced back. Senosi and Luke were watching her. Luke gave her a little wave, but his smile was so sad. Like a little boy being left behind by his parents, trying to be brave.

Senosi was smiling too. He seemed pleased with himself.

Grant's eyes were pretty much glued to the cracks in the treated timbers. He watched as two special ops troops came to take away the unconscious soldier Moth had dropped.

'Looks like Kranz got *bliksemed* by this.' One of the soldiers held up the rock Moth had used. 'Amateur hour – lucky for that muppet. Collins and Adebisi were killed.'

'Rest of the poachers taken care of, bruh,' said the other soldier. 'No sign of Ballantyne, Xai or the rest. The whole mission's gone west.'

'One of the poachers told me that Ballantyne's kids were meant to get here but never arrived.' The woman shrugged. 'Probably killed in the flood.'

'Probably is not good enough. The boss is gonna flip.'

'Maybe that's why the poachers tried to kill us before we could kill them,' said the woman. 'But if the targets are alive, we'll find them from the air.'

The two of them carried Kranz's body away.

'They didn't get Roland, Xai and Niko,' Grant whispered. 'But Robyn . . . Ralph . . .'

'Maybe they found the Bakho,' Moth said. Grant hoped she was right.

They waited until they heard the copter taking off. Grant opened the hinged panel to look outside. 'You may know the land but I don't. Is there somewhere we can go to look over the whole area without standing out?'

140

'Bokmakierie Villa's got the best view,' Moth answered. 'The fanciest guests stay there. It's back up the slope and off to the right.'

Looking all around, Grant followed Moth as she led the way, her catty held up and ready to shoot. Grant saw the bodies of poachers lying on the ground and shuddered.

Soon they reached a spacious wood-fronted building with large windows, nestled elegantly into the landscape.

'Bokmakierie Villa,' Grant murmured. 'The glass hasn't been shot out. That's got to be a good sign, right?'

'But the door's been forced.' Moth pointed. 'Someone got here ahead of us.'

Looking more closely, Grant could see splintered wood in the frame near the front door handle. 'The soldiers would've searched here, I guess,' he said. 'Is there a back way in?'

Moth kept low as she moved past flower beds and ornamental bushes. The back of Bokmakierie Villa was painted yellow with a black stripe clean across it, in honour of the bird it was named for, and the view it enjoyed was of a magical glade with its own burbling brook and a view past mature monkey-puzzle trees. Patio doors led out onto a deck with a large dining table and a brick barbecue area. There was no sign of life, but Grant was glad at least there was no sign of death either.

Abruptly, Moth gave a hoarse, chirruping call. Grant jumped and looked at her. 'What was that?'

'A signal,' Moth said with a smile.

'For your people?' Grant assumed.

'Person,' Moth corrected him, as an answering call rose from the cover of some nearby monkey-puzzles.

The patio door burst open and Xai and Roland darted out, automatic weapons at the ready, and took cover behind the brick barbecue and a large urn respectively. Grant opened his mouth to call to them, but someone else spoke first.

'Jeez, you two!' a deep voice thundered out. 'Trying to scare off an old chommie who only wants to help?' A tall, stocky man with red hair and a scraggy beard strode out from between the tree's spiky branches, holding a high-powered rifle up in one hand to show he was no threat. With two bandoliers strapped in an X across his chest, he looked like he'd wandered out of some old-fashioned revolutionary conflict.

Roland stared at him, slowly lowering his own weapon. 'Yonker,' he breathed. 'Frederick Yonker, so you *are* here!'

'Dad!' Moth called, and ran to him, leaving Grant open-mouthed.

'Motholeli!' Yonker opened his arms and scooped her into a bear hug. 'You fished a politician's son out of the pool, then! Quite a catch, eh?'

Wrong-footed, Grant hurried from the flower bed to join Xai and Roland on the deck. Xai, his wounded arm bandaged now, gave him a slap on the shoulder, and Roland shook his hand.

'Glad you could join us, Grant,' Roland said.

'We've been worried sick,' Niko added, opening a ground-floor window.

Grant started towards the window to embrace her, but

she shrank back as Yonker stepped onto the deck with Moth beside him.

'You!' Niko hissed. 'I saw you in Gauda. You helped them kill all those villagers!'

'Whoa, easy!' Yonker held out his hands to their group. 'It was me who set you free just now, bruh!'

'In Gauda he helped to herd doctors and medics into the community building,' Niko went on, 'so they'd be killed when it was blown to bits!'

Roland raised his weapon in warning. 'I'd hoped there was some mistake here. What is this, Yonker?'

'I'm trying to save your sad backsides, that's what!' Yonker stood in front of Moth protectively. 'Listen, Ballantyne. I took the commission from a man called Shrinker, with no clue that Mbato was involved. I was told we were securing biological weapons on a terrorist site. It was Shrinker who blew Gauda to bits. Mission creep, he told us – we had to contain a virus or millions would die . . .'

'But you didn't contain it,' Grant said, 'did you?'

'He punched me out when I tried to stop him setting the charges, when I realised it was just a town of innocents. Woke up in cuffs when it was all over. Thought they were going to take me out too, but they made threats . . . to her.' He glanced at Moth. 'That was enough to buy my silence.'

'You can't trust him, Roland,' Niko insisted, and Grant was inclined to agree, from all he'd heard. But Moth had helped him escape, and if she trusted Yonker . . .

Yonker's voice hardened. 'Don't you think I'm taking

a chance trusting *you*? I've seen what they've said about you all . . . and I know it's bull. In here, I just know.' He tapped his fingers over his heart and sighed impatiently. 'Look, living so close to Gerhard's place, I've picked up transmissions, signals, all that. I sent all the guests away, broadcast on the radio, saying I was going away, so Mbato wouldn't try to press me into this. When I listened in and heard he was using this place for the pick-up, I knew I had to help. I jemmied your window, Ballantyne, left gear for you – and are you grateful? The hell you are!'

'Why'd you stay hidden?' Grant demanded.

'You think I'm *bossies*? Think I want word getting back to Mbato that I went against him again?' Yonker shook his head. 'Had to clear out so Rontane wouldn't involve me.'

Xai still seemed suspicious. 'Why work for them as a merc when you have this place?'

'Debts! This place didn't come cheap, you know? The banks wouldn't loan me money, so I had to go to the kind of people who would.'

'Loan sharks?' Grant ventured.

'Loan *megalodons*, more like. You know, the big prehistoric great whites, eh?' Yonker saw that no one was smiling along with him, and shrugged. 'Well, anyway, we'd hardly opened when the Covid lockdown kicked in, and things never really got better. But compared to you, well! Even with my livelihood half-blown to hell, I'm having a ball, eh?'

Roland looked at Xai and received a silent nod. He

lowered his gun, and finally he smiled. 'Thanks. I'm sorry your place is trashed.'

Grant relaxed a little as the stand-off ended. Niko still looked uncertain, but Roland gave her a reassuring nod.

'Me too,' said Yonker. 'Well, you can thank me by getting the hell out of here, because believe me, big trouble is coming –'

Niko turned from the window and broke into a coughing fit. She covered her mouth with a hand.

Roland turned to her, concerned. 'Niko?'

'Get away from me.' She lowered her hands, held them out. They were scattered with specks of blood.

'Oh no,' Grant breathed, as Yonker and Moth instinctively took a step back.

'I hoped it was just a cough,' she said softly. 'But Gerhard's virus . . .' A bloody tear rolled down her cheek. 'Maybe my mask was bad. Maybe it was already too late. But I've got the virus too.'

Across the grounds of the Lodge, a steel-blue Land Rover was pulling up outside the shattered reception block. The driver got out and opened the rear door for another man to get out. The man was short with a thick black moustache. He was dressed in a linen suit that might once have been white, but now was grey. The platinum chain around his neck and the rings on his fingers were a bright contrast against his skin.

The man walked over to the body of Kali Rontane, who lay sprawled on the patio amid a million glassy fragments.

'Stop faking it, Rontane,' the man snarled. 'You've never felt dressed without body armour under your clothes.'

Rontane rolled over and glared up at him. 'Those bullets still hit hard enough to break my ribs.'

'Mbato will do worse when he learns you lost our targets. I trusted you to get this right.'

'*You* – trust me?' Rontane spat. 'That's rich. You only cut me in because you were too busy smuggling ivory out of Nampula when Mbato hired you to get Ballantyne.'

'Couldn't miss an opportunity like this, now, could I?' The man smiled thinly, his lips like a crooked scar that ran clear across his face. 'I ought to cut off your ears. Show them to Mbato so he knows you paid the price for letting us down.'

'Big talk!' Rontane sneered. 'Instead of bitching about what we lost, how about we try getting them back? No one knows this land and its hiding places better than you do.'

The man glared down at her. Then he grunted and pulled Rontane to her feet, making her gasp with pain.

'Mbato's special ops force will be out searching for Ballantyne and his pathetic band of brothers now too, so we need to find them first. See which of your guys can still walk and we'll finish this.'

Rontane picked up her fallen cap and glared at him. 'Just like old times, eh?'

'It's for "old times" I said yes to Mbato,' he muttered. 'I want to see Ballantyne's face when he learns that the man who has humbled him – the man who has finally torn him down – is me. Angel Abrafo.'

As Rontane shuffled away to check on the remaining members of her team, Abrafo turned and gazed out over the open sweep of the valley and its game. Where others might find peace and beauty, Abrafo saw only spots for ambush and death for profit. 'Run all you like, Ballantyne,' he breathed. 'As far and fast as you like. You can't hide from me. After all these years, I'm finally going to end you.'

19

At Bokmakierie Villa, Grant watched anxiously as Niko slumped in a chair in the downstairs room. He turned to Roland, Xai and Yonker. 'There must be something we can do to help.'

Yonker didn't look hopeful. 'Our last guests brought the virus here – two women. The first fell sick so quickly. They chartered a helicopter to take them to a private clinic across the border in Zimbabwe. We couldn't help them here.'

Niko had overheard. 'There was nothing I could do for my patients in Gauda either.'

'But the virus has spread now. The world will have moved fast on this, right?' Grant argued. 'There could be new therapies, enough to slow its progress at least . . .'

Grant saw the lines in Roland's face deepen. He looked utterly desolate. Grant remembered the grief in Robyn's voice when she'd described her mother's death, and guessed that Roland was picturing the same thing happening again, right here. With an effort that was obvious to Grant but hidden from the others standing further away, Roland regained

148

his calm expression. 'Grant's right,' he said. 'If only we can get you –'

'To a private clinic in Zimbabwe?' Niko said softly. 'I don't think so.'

'Perhaps my people could help,' Xai said. 'Yonker, you know these parts better than anyone. We've been trying to find any last pockets of the Bakho.'

'They're long gone. Driven out when the miners were given the land,' Yonker said. 'Some were killed for trying to stand up to Mbato – like Moth's folks. When that happened, I took her in.'

'The Bakho are still out there, though,' Moth said. 'In their place of hiding. I know it.'

Yonker gave her a look. 'We've been through this, sweetheart. I've always encouraged you to find out about your heritage –'

'They *are* out there!' Moth insisted. 'I've seen a woman, sometimes. And a man older than you. I've worked out the places where their camp might be hidden – out-of-the-way places, easy to defend –'

'Could you show us on a map?' Grant asked her. When the others looked at him, clearly not inclined to believe her, he shrugged. 'If nothing else, we could use someplace hard to find and easy to defend, couldn't we?'

Roland scowled. 'We need real intelligence to go on.'

Moth bristled.

'You haven't seen how capable Moth is,' Grant put in.

'I *can* show you the sites where they might be,' Moth said fiercely. 'I've spent months searching.'

Yonker reacted like he'd been sucker-punched. 'Why didn't you tell me?'

Moth looked down at the floor, angrily wiping at her eyes. 'I just . . .'

'Blood ties are strong,' said Xai, and placed a hand on Yonker's shoulder while looking kindly at the girl. 'I can't believe the Bakho would give up on their ancestral lands, either,' he said, crouching down beside her. 'Roland, let me check her maps. In any case, Grant's right – we can't stay here. We could use a safe hideout.'

'All right,' said Roland. 'You do that. Yonker, if soldiers or poachers come back in force, can we defend ourselves?'

Yonker hesitated. 'I've got transport hidden away down the hillside. We can take that and drive to this cache of combat supplies I keep hidden down in the valley. In our line of work, you stay prepared. Because *who prepares, wins*. The Ballantyne motto. Right?'

'Right,' Roland agreed. 'But I'm not your commanding officer any more. I have no right to ask you to risk your –'

'Oh, spare me, bruh!' said Yonker. 'You know I'm in.'

'Dad,' Moth hissed suddenly, and he fell silent. In the distance, voices were carrying.

'Please, Rontane, my leg . . .'

'Get up, you miserable jackal! You'll get no payback lying in the dirt.'

'Sounds like the Queen of the Poachers made it,' Grant muttered.

'And she's not alone,' Moth agreed.

'Yonker, we'd better get these maps,' said Xai.

'While you do that, Dad, I can prep the jeep,' Moth said. 'Maybe Grant could come with me?'

Grant nodded. 'Sure.'

'All right,' said Yonker. 'We'll follow with Niko once we've rigged a stretcher, eh?'

'Be careful,' Roland said. 'And good luck.'

Good luck, thought Grant grimly. *Sure. Maybe in the next life.*

Robyn wasn't sure how long she'd been asleep this time, but she was back lying in bed in the strange hospital room carved out of the rock. She was feeling less dizzy now, and focused on Senosi as he poured various solutions into beakers and test tubes in a small lab area in the corner, lit by a battered old Anglepoise lamp.

'Welcome back,' Senosi said without turning around.

'I can't believe Luke is alive . . .' She frowned. 'Do you know any more about my brother? Has anyone in the tribe seen him?'

'Not yet. But our hunters are all around the area. He may be sighted.' Senosi paused. 'Besides concern for your family, how are you feeling now?'

Robyn stretched and winced. 'My arm is sore.'

'Ah. Sorry, that's me making a pincushion of it.'

'Blood tests?'

'Samples. Your blood is very unusual, Robyn. And luckily for you, it's combined with elements of our natural medicines in a most unexpected way.'

'Luckily, as in I'm still alive,' Robyn reasoned. She paused to think. 'I have a genetic quirk from my dad that helps my immune system resist viruses. I fought off Ebola when I was young. We all caught it. Dad, my brother and I all got through OK. But Mum died.'

'She lacked the immunity passed down from your father, of course,' Senosi said gently. 'This virus is interesting. Some people catch it quickly, while others seem to have more resistance. But *your* resistance . . .' He whistled. 'Well, we need to isolate your plasma and antibodies, but the early signs are promising.'

'Promising?'

'That there is hope for a cure. Something that offers my people hope also.'

'Sorry?' Robyn sat up in bed, feeling sick. 'You mean, I've passed on the virus to your people?'

'No, no. Don't distress yourself. I mean, were we to find a way to help the world's population recover from this virus, think of the gratitude we would earn.'

Robyn looked at him. 'Gratitude's all you want?'

'Oh, we can name our price, I know. But money is no help to my people. The land is. Belonging is.' Senosi's voice had hardened. 'You think I take liberties, perhaps? It is *your* blood I have used, after all. Your people have taken lands from the Bakho and peoples like us time and time again, and exploited them without consent. Now you must think I am doing the same to you.'

'I have never hurt your people,' Robyn told him truly. 'I've grown up with a wonderful Bakho tracker, a man called Xai, and he's like a second parent to me. He's educated me in so many ways. If my blood can help you and the wider world, of course you should use it.'

'I remember your friend, Xai. He left us long ago, but he did not return as I did.' Senosi gave a stiff little bow. 'I'm sorry, Robyn. I have spent so much of my life torn between two worlds – playing the part of the sangoma here and a lawyer in the world outside, sneaking between the two so as not to draw attention to our being here, while trying to improve my people's lot as best I can . . .'

'A lawyer?' Robyn looked at Senosi's bright, geometrically patterned clothes and tried to picture him in a sober suit; it made her smile. 'I suppose your people really need to know their rights and stuff. With all that's been taken from you.'

'Shame I wasn't qualified twenty years ago,' Senosi said. 'I could have helped my father fight Mbato in the courts, and this area might still be filled with Bakho. Just as it was before we were evicted from our homelands by the man who would one day become your great president . . . so he could rip apart the veldt for mining.'

'Mbato owns mines?' Robyn frowned.

'Most of them are spent and empty now, but yes, he owned many mines,' Senosi explained. 'It's said that while he was in the army he made a fortune by helping a poaching gang traffic ivory.'

'And I know whose gang.' Robyn felt a sneer twist her features. 'Angel Abrafo.'

'You know of Abrafo.' Senosi nodded. 'Of course, your father fought in the same unit as Mbato, and in the Lebombo Mountains.'

153

'*You* know a lot about us,' Robyn noted.

'The state news is full of the crimes you're supposed to have committed,' Senosi said.

Just an observation, Robyn wondered, *or a deliberate change of subject?*

'Ironic, isn't it? The world thinks your family started this pandemic, when in fact you may hold the key to ending it.'

'I'm glad you don't believe that stuff on the news.'

'Mbato controls the media. And after all Luke has told us about him and Gerhard, we know that nothing about them is what it seems.'

'That works both ways.' Robyn watched as the lawyer/sangoma busied himself with technology she could only guess at. 'Most people think the Bakho are simple hunter gatherers, and look at all you're doing.'

'We break the stereotype, you mean. That's the only reason a few of us were able to maintain our community here,' said Senosi grimly. 'Here, on land that holds nothing beneath it but the red ochre our ancestors mined for the cave drawings you see on the walls. Nothing of value to the mining corporations.' With a soft chuckle, he shook his head. 'It suits us that those with power underestimate us. How could "primitives" like the Bakho bother one so powerful as Mbato or Josef Gerhard?'

'Gerhard,' Robyn said sharply. 'He's the man who created this virus. He took wild animals, twisted their DNA and created ancient predators, like cave lions. He dragged that virus into the world. He tried to have Luke killed . . .'

Senosi held up a hand to calm her. 'And yet Luke says that Gerhard sent drones to scare away the beasts that hunted him, and had his staff stitch up Luke's wounds.'

Robyn blinked. 'Why would he say that?'

'Luke's father is another of those clever, powerful people we discussed. Luke claims that Gerhard planned to use him to force Mr van Rok into helping with some business scheme or other . . .' Senosi studied a test tube and nodded with satisfaction. 'Still. Don't distress yourself with thoughts of Gerhard. You're safe here. That's what matters.'

'No,' Robyn said sourly. 'What matters is my brother is somewhere out there and I can't reach him. I've got to help him.'

'You are helping us here,' Senosi reminded her. 'Just as we have helped you. A fair bargain, no? You will stay a little longer, please.'

Robyn bit her lip as Senosi left the room. Was anyone really looking for Ralph? she wondered. Or were they just trying to stop her complaining while they bled the life from her?

That's not fair, she told herself. But she felt uneasy.

She caught a shadow of furtive movement in the doorway. Fear gripped her throat for a second until she saw it was Luke.

'Don't say anything,' he whispered. Looking all around, he slipped into the room and stood in the shadows near the equipment. 'Listen to me. We've got to get out of here.'

'And find Ralph,' Robyn agreed. 'Yes, I know, but I can't just –'

'No, I said *listen*.' Luke cut her off. 'This set-up is a sham. Senosi isn't who you think he is. He's working for Gerhard!'

20

It was a relief for Ralph when they reached the unassuming wooden building that stood in the centre of the mine workings. The sun had been beating down relentlessly and his face felt sore and tight with sunburn, so it was a relief to feel the shade. Best of all, the two titanoboas remained outside, swaying, while Gerhard ushered Ralph in through the door.

'We need to work on the titanoboas' locomotion – drive them harder and further over long distances.' Gerhard thrust the tablet at one of his assistants. 'Stimulate the adrenal gland, really hurt them. We'll see if pain speeds them up.' He cuffed Ralph around the face, making him gasp. 'The pain response is very helpful when you need an animal to do what you want.' He turned back to the assistant. 'Get on with it.'

The man nodded, looking doubtful, but he kept any concerns he may have had to himself as he left with his colleague and the door closed behind him.

That just leaves one snake to deal with, thought Ralph,

rubbing his bruised cheek. *The most dangerous of all.* He allowed himself the fantasy of overpowering Gerhard, pictured smashing his balding head against a table and making his escape. But, weakened as he was from thirst and hunger, where would he escape to? The titanoboa sentries, the high fence, the massive expanse of wilderness . . . Even if he had the strength, where could he go?

I mustn't give up, Ralph told himself. *I need to find a chance and make the most of it.* Looking around, he realised that once this room must have been a canteen and a meeting space for the mine workers. Now it was as dusty and neglected as all the other places he'd explored. The food counter was piled with rusting utensils.

'Lunch time?' Ralph said. 'What are you gonna do – mess with the DNA of some old crumbs and bring them back as a three-course meal?'

Gerhard smiled languidly, pulled a small flask from his pocket, swigged and swallowed smugly. 'You must be wondering why. Why would Josef Gerhard, who owns thousands of square kilometres of prime African national parkland, locate anything here in this inconvenient dump?'

Ralph hadn't been wondering that – he had more important things to think about – but he'd bite, if only to keep Gerhard talking while he worked on his plan. 'Maybe you had this place before you moved next door to us,' Ralph suggested. 'Maybe you inherited this old mine from some prospector in your family.'

'Good reasoning, Ralph.' Gerhard actually looked impressed. 'In fact, this mine belonged to our great president.'

Ralph frowned. 'Mbato?'

'He earned enough blood money during his army days to buy the land. Land that is rich in cobalt. No doubt you know that rechargeable batteries need cobalt . . . and Gerhard Industries needed a lot of rechargeable batteries. So I invested in his mine.'

'The start of a sick friendship,' muttered Ralph.

'A fruitful one.' Gerhard held out the flask to him.

Ralph was so, so thirsty, but he hesitated. Could he trust Gerhard? Just as he reached out for the drink, Gerhard tipped the flask and poured the contents onto the floor. Ralph watched the liquid soak into the dusty floorboards.

'He who hesitates is lost,' Gerhard murmured. 'In life, as in business.'

Ralph stared at him hatefully. *Just wait till I have a shot at you*, he thought darkly. *I won't hesitate then.*

'Of course, once the mine had been worked dry, I had parts of it . . . repurposed. By then, you see, I'd become interested in the research of a Danish science team who'd recreated the sarcosuchus. The area around here is rich in well-preserved fossils and organic material from prehistory.'

Ralph thought of the turtle shell he'd found. Why couldn't Gerhard have brought that back instead of giant snakes?

'Where better to set up a genetic research facility far from the tedious watchful eyes of those old fools at the Department of Science and Technology?'

'They'd have stopped you. All the animals you must have tortured and killed, splicing ancient DNA into their genes –'

'They died so that their extinct ancestors might live,'

Gerhard argued. 'A purposeful death to crown an otherwise pointless existence.' He crossed to the counter and reached beneath it, searching for something. There was a click, and then a hatch opened in the floor, making a grinding noise. In the soft glow it emitted Ralph could see the top of a ladder.

'As you've observed, I've enjoyed a good deal of success with my little experiments.' Gerhard produced a small gun and waved it towards the ladder. 'Care to explore?'

Ralph felt afraid at the idea of descending into whatever hell Gerhard had devised beneath them. 'Why do you even want to show me?'

'I require your assistance.' Gerhard gestured to the hatch again. 'Move.'

A little unsteadily, Ralph climbed down the ladder. He considered trying to drop down and run out of sight, but he had no idea what to expect down here, and Gerhard would know the place like the back of his hand. *Get some local knowledge*, he told himself. *Then maybe you can get out again.*

'I still don't see why you're so obsessed with making predasaurs in real life instead of just in virtual reality,' Ralph said, hoping that if he kept Gerhard talking the man would give away something useful.

'Don't you indeed.' Gerhard scoffed softly. 'When Mbato achieves his third term, he will legalise my predasaurs as the ultimate big game hunt. People will pay anything – anything!' Gerhard gestured with the gun, shepherding Ralph to take a left turn. 'Then Mbato will legalise the trade in ivory – ivory that is harvested from my mammoths and woolly rhinos *only*, beasts that are my property, bred for this purpose and with no rights to protection or conservation because I can clone them with ease . . .'

Ralph turned on Gerhard. 'Do you not hear yourself? You think it's OK to exploit living animals –'

'Living only because I willed it.' Gerhard looked irritated. 'You're not using your intelligence, Ralph. More hunters coming for my predasaurs means less slaughter of big game, correct? And when my ivory is legal to trade, poacher scum like Rontane and Abrafo and their criminal gangs will no longer be able to profit.'

Ralph narrowed his eyes in grim understanding. 'Because *you'll* be the only one profiting.'

'And why shouldn't I? I'll be doing more to protect animals than your tedious father ever could.'

'Don't make out that you're doing it for the animals. You want to *control* them,' said Ralph, 'to direct them. In games and in real life.' He watched Gerhard closely. 'All these fingers in so many pies. But what's it all leading to, Gerhard? What's the endgame?'

'The endgame?' Gerhard said lightly. 'That's none of your concern. This virus, on the other hand? That most certainly is your concern – or rather, the way I intend to rid the world of it is.'

'How?'

'You should be asking, *who*?' Gerhard grinned. 'Oh, yes, Ralph. I was wise to spare you. A little bird tells me that Ballantyne blood has uncanny resistance to the virus.'

Ralph swallowed. 'I don't believe you.'

'Your sister would appear to be proof.'

His stomach dropped. 'Robyn? Will you tell me where she is?'

Gerhard nodded. 'And I'll tell you *what* she is – the means to a cure that could save the world. Think how well-disposed the world will be to the man who saved millions of lives. Instant celebrity. Instant access to the biggest names in business and tech research. Gerhard Industries will become a top-ten multinational, years ahead of my original schedule. And my endgame will move all the faster towards completion.' He jabbed the gun against Ralph's spine. 'Turning negatives into positives – that's what life's all about, isn't it?'

Ralph gritted his teeth. 'I asked you, *where is Robyn*?'

'Where you'd expect her to be,' Gerhard said. 'In as much trouble as you are.'

'Senosi is working for *Gerhard*?' Robyn's voice fell to a whisper, ground out through gritted teeth, but still it seemed to fill the hospital cell. 'How do you know?'

'The Bakho here aren't your regular tribe,' he began. 'They're advanced. Crazy advanced.'

'Of course they are, you're standing in front of their medical tech –'

'Not just this stuff!' Luke hissed. 'These hidden caves must stretch for miles, like a bunker beneath the mountains. And there's wifi – a special network. I have my phone, see, and they think I just play games on it –'

Robyn frowned. 'I thought that was taken off you at Gerhard's complex?'

'Duh, it was. But when I came round from my operation, that ranger, Abi, was on the couch beside me. She said you'd saved her life.'

Robyn nodded slowly, remembering. 'I did. She's all right, then?'

'She pulled through, and thank God she did, and thank God you made that happen, cos she's not as much of a hard-nosed old cow now. She even let me have my phone to game on while I recuperated. I mean, she dumped the security apps first, obvs, so I couldn't get up to anything . . .' He smiled. 'But what Abi *didn't* know was that I had an app on there that recovers anything that's been deleted! I got back the security stuff, hacked my way into Gerhard's security and escaped on a trail bike . . .'

'While you were so injured?' Robyn was impressed. 'How'd you manage to cover so many miles without Gerhard finding you?'

'Because he'd already sent everyone after you,' said Luke. 'I rode. Walked. Climbed. Wounds got infected, though. When the Bakho found me and treated me, I thought my luck had changed, but . . .'

'Go on,' said Robyn.

'Well, I've been stuck here. I wanted to get out. Talk to my parents at least, you know? That nice Bakho lady here who helped you, she let me charge my phone and of course I hacked into the San's private network, trying to send a message to my dad. Turns out I can't get a call through to the world outside, but I *can* listen in on the calls that come and go in and out of here. And I heard Senosi . . . talking to Gerhard.'

'No way,' Robyn breathed.

'Yes way. Senosi told Gerhard how your immune system took care of the virus. It's not him who wants a cure for it, it's Gerhard.'

A chill swept over Robyn. 'You mean, Senosi is using my blood to help *him*?'

'That's right,' Luke whispered. 'I mean, I know these guys have great tech, but do you think they set this up on their own? Can you really imagine a Bakho tribe developing a brand-new vaccine – from some secret caves in the mountains?'

Robyn had wanted so much to believe Senosi. But Luke's words made the whole idea seem ridiculous. 'Luke, are you totally sure it was Gerhard –'

'That's why he's not sent anyone to get me, Robyn – he knows Senosi will hand me over to him whenever he's ready.' Luke grimaced. 'There's more, too . . .'

'What?'

'Your brother,' Luke said. 'Last I heard, Gerhard had spotted him near this old mine where he films *Predasaur*.'

Hope rushed through Robyn in a golden wave, fast followed by fear for Ralph. 'Did Gerhard get him?'

'I don't know.'

'Oh God,' Robyn breathed. 'Luke, we have to find him before Gerard does!'

'Right!' he agreed. 'Meaning we have to get away from here, which is what I said in the first place.'

164

She nodded. 'But how are we gonna find a way out?'

'I got hold of this.' Luke showed her his phone screen, and Robyn saw a map of what looked like tunnels with rooms leading off.

'Is that this place?' she asked.

Luke nodded and tapped one room on the screen. 'X marks the spot. There's an emergency exit, a staircase cut into the rock leading all the way to the surface . . . if you're strong enough to take it?'

'I'll manage,' Robyn said with cold certainty. 'Anger is an energy. And I'm ready to use it.'

21

Grant was impressed; Yonker and Moth had concealed their emergency jeep well. First they'd dug a broad pit about a metre deep with a sloping ramp at one end, floored and reinforced with wooden boards so the tyres would have grip. Then a dark tarpaulin had been placed over the top of the jeep and sandy soil piled over it. Grasses and creepers threaded carefully through green cargo netting made a near-impenetrable curtain around the jeep, and saplings planted all around helped screen everything even more. A huge termite mound had been built up next to the jeep, adding to the cover.

Niko lay on the ground on the stretcher; Roland and Xai had carried her most of the way along the treacherous path down the mountain. She watched them now, looking tired and sweaty, as Moth crossed to a mighty torchwood tree and tugged hard on a creeper. There was a rustling in the crowning branches and, when she heaved again, a plastic bundle slipped noisily into sight. One more tug and the bundle came loose, crashing to the forest floor.

Inside the thick plastic wrap, Grant could see spades and shovels.

'How long is it since you left the jeep here?' asked Roland.

'Must be two years,' said Yonker, surveying the site. 'Pity to have to uproot these termites.'

'But, since Moth's work with the maps checks out,' said Xai, bestowing a kindly smile on her, 'needs must.'

Moth's shy smile in response flashed across her face like a sunbeam. Grant felt its warmth as he stepped forward to help Moth open the bundle of shovels.

'We'll take care of excavation duties,' Yonker said. 'Grant, Moth, get to higher ground and keep a lookout for soldiers and poachers. We need to be sure we're not drawing attention.'

Moth scurried away immediately, and Grant jogged after her up a steep slope. Soon they had reached an outcrop ringed by knobthorn trees. Some branches had been broken off to carve out a space, a kind of natural fortified turret with fair visibility of the terrain in all directions.

'You watch out north and east,' said Grant, as Moth slipped a stone in her catty. 'I'll take south and west.'

He gazed out over the rippling landscape, where the gentle hills slowly rose and fell towards the great vegetated sand dunes on the distant shore of the Indian Ocean. *Robyn, Ralph*, he thought, *where are you?*

The grunt and squeal of wildebeest drew his eye to a watering hole below them. He watched as the wildebeest clustered with zebra and nyala to drink: safety in numbers, clearly, as Grant could make out a lioness atop an anthill, watching the proceedings with interest. But from here Grant could also see what the herbivores could not: a leopard, so much closer, in the branches of a tree, biding its time and watching for unwary stragglers.

It was a useful lesson. *Prey or predator*, Grant reflected. *You have to be sure you're watching the right thing.*

'Where's this cache of weapons, then?' Grant asked.

'There.' Moth pointed ahead. 'Dad's sent me to check it's not been disturbed so many times. It was while I was out there looking around that I found this old path . . .' She shrugged. 'It might lead to a Bakho hideout. I tried to find a way through, but the path was unpassable. Until I'm bigger and stronger, anyway.'

'Couldn't your dad help you look?' Grant asked.

'I . . . didn't want to upset him.' Moth looked downcast. 'Didn't want him to think I was trying to leave him. We're all each other has. My parents were killed in a . . . convenient accident while protesting outside one of Mbato's mines. My whole family, dead and gone. If Dad hadn't found me . . .'

'Didn't he try to return you to your people?'

'Like a lost parcel?' Moth's large, dark eyes bored into his. 'My tribe was scattered. It's not like he's tried to hold me back from my heritage – Dad always encouraged me to get to know the lands that my family came from. Their culture and stuff. You know?' She looked out across the mountains, the breeze ruffling her dark hair. 'And yeah, I can read about it, watch videos, look at pictures . . . but I can't *feel* it. I still don't really know what I am. Does that make any sense?'

Grant nodded. 'I get it. My whole life, my dad was grooming me for a life in politics, to follow him into the party. But I don't know if I want that.' He paused. 'Maybe your dad prefers to believe the Bakho are all gone. Because if you find them, he's afraid he'll lose you.'

Moth looked at him. 'You shouldn't be a politician. You talk sense.'

They kept watch in silence, but it was companionable rather than awkward. Grant watched the last light of day darken into a golden-tinged purple. The tops of the trees lining the river still showed touches of movement: mopane and acacia leaves fluttered in the breeze. Cicadas and crickets hummed and chirped among the tall grasses lining the riverbank. Reed frogs and nightjars added their calls to the evening sounds.

Then the sound of an engine firing carried through the air.

'They've got the jeep working!' Grant beamed.

But the next moment, a gunshot rang out, its echo cracking off the bare branches. His stomach twisting with fear, Grant stared all around, but he couldn't see any sign of an enemy. Moth pushed past him, her catty raised, and moved like a gazelle back along the wooded trail.

'Moth, wait!' Grant hissed. But she was already out of sight.

As quietly as he could, Grant made his way down towards the little clearing. He had to see what was happening.

And when he did, he felt cold through to his soul.

The jeep had been unearthed but now a poacher stood in the clearing; a lean young man that Rontane had called Malik, Grant recalled. Malik looked beaten and bruised but his gun covered Roland, Xai and Yonker. Niko lay on her stretcher, pale and sweaty, her eyes closed.

A lazy voice sounded from the treeline. 'So, Ballantyne . . . his little rogue, Xai . . . and Yonker, too! What a reunion.'

The man who'd spoken sauntered into sight. The gaudy platinum chain around his neck and linen suit were testament to wealth worn cheaply. But despite his short stature he looked powerful, and this image was enhanced by the knives and guns he had holstered in his thick leather belt.

Roland just stared at the newcomer. He spat out two words like they were poison in his mouth: 'Angel Abrafo.'

Ralph had started off making careful note of the turns he'd been forced to take through Gerhard's underground complex; the doors they'd gone through, the scuffs on the wall, any cracks or stains that might make useful markers on the journey back out of here. But truth was, all the corridors looked the same, and he was tired, and dehydrated, and his concentration was as shot as his confidence.

Gerhard, still driving Ralph forward at gunpoint, paused for a moment and pressed his thumb against some kind of scanner in the wall. There was a beep and a green LED bulb winked on beside the scanner. Then double doors at the end of the corridor slid open for them.

'After you,' said Gerhard with exaggerated politeness.

Ralph stepped through into a warehouse-sized space beyond. The change in atmosphere was immediate: warm air caught in his nostrils, carrying the smell of animal dung, cut vegetation and over-ripe fruit. The metal walkway was flanked by animal pens. He could hear harsh breathing, and the scrape of claws on concrete.

Oh, God, there's predasaurs in here, Ralph thought grimly. *He's gonna feed me to them.*

A woman emerged from between two cages holding a mop. With a shock, Ralph realised he recognised her – it was one of Gerhard's rangers.

'Abi,' he said.

A blonde-haired bully with a buzz cut, Abi had caught him and Robyn and Luke trespassing, and had not been gentle when it came to subduing them. When Ralph had seen her last, she'd been badly hurt by one of the predasaurs. Sure enough, she was limping, leaning on the mop like it was a crutch. Her right hip was clearly bandaged beneath her white overalls.

'So. Back, then,' said Abi, dark eyes fixed on him.

Ralph struggled for a good comeback. 'Not through choice,' he said.

'No one gets away from Gerhard,' she said. It was meant to be a gloat, he supposed, but it sounded weary, as if she knew from her own experience.

'Good to see you're back on your feet,' said Ralph. It was Robyn who'd helped Abi with her injuries, perhaps saved her life. Maybe she'd show a scintilla of gratitude – maybe she'd help him? *Yeah, right,* he thought.

'Abi, you're relieved of clean-up duties,' Gerhard said. 'I need your assistance with Ralph here. He needs rehydration – the special carbohydrate solution.'

Abi nodded slowly and left, still using the mop as a crutch.

'I'm guessing that Gerhard Industries' sick leave isn't so good,' Ralph observed. 'She looks bad.'

'My staff has been somewhat depleted since you and your family left my reserve in such a mess, Ralph. Given the circumstances, I've had to reallocate roles. I'm sure you'll appreciate that a cure must be found for your virus.'

Ralph bristled at the 'your', and was about to put up a fight, but Gerhard gestured he should keep moving along the walkway. So Ralph walked on, more thirsty than ever now that Gerhard had mentioned a drink.

He jumped as something large and dark slammed into the bars of its cage, towering over him on its hind legs: a giant short-faced bear. Its red eyes burned with hatred and it snarled at him, saliva flicking from its jaws as it shook its head. He turned from it and kept on walking. Ralph hated seeing the animals in Gerhard's cages. He knew they suffered intense pain caused by the patchwork of modern and ancient genetics stitched together by Gerard's scientists.

But then he passed a young woolly rhino. Its eyes were pink, not the raw bloodshot red of other predasaurs.

Ralph looked from the rhino to Gerhard. 'This one is different from the others?'

'Sometimes nature attempts to reassert itself over the artificial improvements I have bestowed upon these beasts,' Gerhard said loftily. 'It's helpful, really. By studying this one we can see which genes code its more placid nature . . .'

'And remove them,' said Ralph bitterly.

'Of course.' Gerhard turned at the sound of uneven

footsteps along the walkway. 'Ah, dear, loyal Abi is catching us up. She'll join us through here.'

Ralph was about to ask 'Where?' when a pair of doors opened in front of him at the end of the walkway to reveal a sterile white space with a couple of men in scrubs inside. From them, and from the pens he could see, Ralph assumed it was a room where the animals were given medical treatment – or opened up and taken apart, cell by cell, to improve their predatory natures.

Abi caught up with them at last. She was carrying a small tray. Ralph turned, eager for his drink.

All he saw was a syringe.

The two men in scrubs grabbed him by the arms. Ralph struggled, tried to kick, but he couldn't break free. They held out his left arm as Abi prepared the syringe and injected clear fluid into his arm. The sharp scratch made him wince.

'Don't be concerned, Ralph,' Gerhard said. 'It's a solution designed to stimulate the production of certain proteins in your blood. Comparing yours with your sister's should be quite instructive.'

Ralph gasped as the men bundled him roughly into a padded chair with arm rests and an open back and fastened his wrists and ankles with soft restraints. 'What are you doing?'

'Just relax. The nurses here are going to take some blood samples and cerebrospinal fluid, perform some serologic antibody tests, and measure the target antibodies, proteins and antigens. It shouldn't take too long to prepare samples of convalescent plasma,' Gerhard went on genially. 'Then all we'll need for testing is someone suitably unwell.'

Ralph strained against his restraints, but they didn't give a millimetre. 'If you need someone sick, just look in the mirror.'

Gerhard's smile grew a little tighter. 'We'll begin with a lumbar puncture, I think, Nurse. Hold still, Ralph.'

The words made Ralph go cold.

The nurse nodded. 'I'll apply the iodine.'

Ralph winced as his shirt was tugged up and the liquid was brushed over his back. Then he saw the size of the needle and closed his eyes. *Don't scream*, he told himself. *Don't scream and give Gerhard the satisfaction . . .*

He was still thinking it when the needle was inserted between his vertebrae, and sharp pain lanced through him. A bellow was ripped from his lungs.

It wasn't the last.

22

'*Abrafo*.' Roland Ballantyne said the name aloud, and it reverberated through Grant's brain. At the mere mention of the poacher overlord, Grant knew how high the stakes were.

A reckoning between these men had always been on the cards. Roland had lost good friends and comrades to Abrafo: he had been seeking vengeance for twenty years. All Abrafo had lost was cash, a supply route and a blind eye to his business, but in his book Grant supposed that must weigh the same. As they stared each other out like rival lions, wanting to dominate the other, you could almost smell the testosterone in the air.

Malik kept his gun trained on Yonker and Xai while Abrafo pulled a revolver from his belt and pointed it at Ballantyne. 'Seems like only yesterday that I massacred your unit, eh? But these lands, they've changed so much. Almost beyond recognition. Whereas you . . . you're just as dumb as ever.' Abrafo smiled smugly. 'It's got to sting, boys, huh? I beat you back then – and now here I am, doing it again.'

Grant stifled a gasp as a hand slipped over his mouth from behind.

It was Moth. With her other hand she forced her catapult and several stones into his sweaty palm. 'Used one of these before?' she whispered.

Grant nodded. 'I'm a good shot.'

'Aim for heads. On my signal.'

'What signal?'

'You'll know.' As quickly and quietly as she'd arrived, Moth departed, swallowed by the undergrowth, and Grant's attention shifted back to the drama playing out below.

'It makes sense that Mbato would use you, Abrafo,' said Roland. 'It was him that warned you we were coming for you back then, wasn't it?'

'And I paid him well for it,' Abrafo agreed. 'Now he's returning the favour. What goes around comes around.'

Rontane stepped out of the cover, her gold teeth catching the last of the sunlight. Grant fumbled to put a stone in the catty. Where was Moth? What was the signal going to be?

'So.' Rontane waved her gun between Ballantyne and Yonker. 'Which of you opened fire on Mbato's helicopter?'

'It was me,' Roland said. 'Oh, did they think it was you? Sorry.'

'Clever strategy. But high-risk.' She pointed the gun at his kneecap. 'And that risk hasn't paid off.'

Grant gripped the catty more tightly, sweat trickling down his back. *Come on, Moth* . . .

'Don't hurt him yet,' Abrafo ordered, pointing to Niko on the stretcher, who looked pale and breathless.

'Yeah,' Malik growled. 'We've already got one of them to carry.'

Xai shook his head. 'Aren't you worried that Mbato's troops will kill you on sight before you hand us over?'

'I've radioed Mbato. Explained the . . . misunderstanding.'

'And you think he'll actually pay you now instead of killing you?' Roland sounded disbelieving. 'As for you, Rontane, after your mess-up, you think Abrafo's going to give you anything more than a bullet in the back?'

'Come on, Ballantyne!' Rontane sneered, stalking to stand between Abrafo and Malik. 'Trying to turn us against each other? That's so predictable.'

The *korr-korr* of a bird sounded from high up in the branches. Grant tensed. Was that the signal, or just a turaco? No, back at the Lodge, Moth had made a different bird call . . .

Abrafo's grin was growing larger and smugger. 'You military *domkops* can't out-think me. I mean, Yonker, for God's sake – you think I didn't know you had this jeep hidden here? I knew you'd go for it now.'

'Well . . .' Yonker looked sharply from Malik down to the ground. 'If you've chosen to stand there, you can't know what's gonna happen next . . .'

The ground under Malik heaved with swift movement. Rontane grabbed Abrafo and pulled him clear as a stretch of cargo netting, concealed by leaf cover on the forest floor, was gathered up into a net. Malik was lifted, struggling, into the air. He fired his automatic weapon, raking the clearing with gunfire.

That's a signal, all right, Grant decided. He raised the catty, pulled back the elastic band and fired his rock. The gunfire stopped as Malik was struck and went limp.

Then everything seemed to happen at once. Roland stooped to grab Niko from the stretcher as Xai threw open the rear door to the jeep. Yonker jumped into the driver's seat and turned the key in the ignition. Abrafo swung his gun up to fire, but Grant shot a second strike from Moth's catty and knocked the gun from his hand. It would have been the shot of his life if he hadn't actually been aiming for Abrafo's head.

Yonker gunned the engine, and Grant broke cover to jump down into the clearing. While Xai got Niko safely inside, Roland ran at Abrafo. But Rontane had recovered and her gun was in her hand. She shot at Roland, but Malik, still bundled up in the net, swung into the path of the bullet. Rontane aimed at Roland's legs instead, but Roland jumped up and clung to the net, Malik's bleeding body shielding him. His heart pounding, Grant fired off a third stone that skimmed Rontane's forehead, spoiling her aim. At the same time, Moth ran from cover and whacked Rontane around the head with a tree branch before bringing it down on the back of Abrafo's skull. He gasped and fell forward, dazed.

'Get in!' Roland shouted, jumping down from the net and clambering in beside Yonker. Xai threw open the rear doors and Moth and Grant piled inside. They were barely seated before Yonker had the jeep in gear and was revving away, up the ramp and out of the shallow pit. Malik's body in the net slammed against the windscreen as they drove forward. Yonker swerved towards Abrafo, but the poacher king rolled out of the way and fired after them. Tiny fracture lines cracked across the rear windscreen as the laminated safety glass took the impact of the bullets.

The jeep piled on over the rough terrain, shaking everyone like a plane hitting turbulence. Xai had to cling to Niko to stop her falling off the rear seat. They'd got maybe five hundred metres when Moth pointed through the windscreen to a steel-blue Land Rover. 'More poachers up ahead!'

'Holding back here so Abrafo and Rontane could creep up on foot and surprise you,' Grant guessed.

Luckily there were only two men in the vehicle. They leaned out of the windows, aiming their rifles, ready to open fire. Yonker drove straight for the Land Rover and yanked the handbrake up as he swung the wheel hard clockwise. They side-swiped the vehicle, giving it a vicious impact that knocked the poachers flying before they could fire. Then Yonker accelerated again and they were bumping away downhill. Tree branches clawed at the sides of the jeep and battered at the windscreen – nature's little hands trying to fight their way inside. Grant realised he was holding his breath, desperate to escape.

And suddenly they were free. There was space around them, as if they'd just burst out of a tunnel. But ahead was a perilous escarpment that looked as if it ended in a sheer drop. Yonker threw the wheel hard left and sent the jeep hurtling down another track.

'The weapons are a couple of miles from here,' Moth reported.

'Abrafo said he knew about the jeep being hidden here,' said Grant. 'What if he knows about the weapons too? We could be driving into an ambush!'

23

Keep going, Robyn told herself. It felt like she and Luke had been trekking through the bushveld for hours. The heat made Robyn feel dizzy, and having Luke beside her was giving her vivid flashbacks to the predasaur hunt they'd endured.

The more she staggered on through the long grass, the more nothing seemed to make sense. She and Luke had escaped Senosi's care with no real difficulty; they'd ducked back into alcoves in the cave walls whenever anyone had passed, and once outside the Bakho had only half-heartedly tried to make them return. There was no anger in the people's faces, only confusion and concern.

'Senosi's brainwashed them all,' Luke said. 'They don't know their wise leader is doing a deal with Gerhard.'

'But surely,' Robyn began, 'Senosi would have put guards on us if he was keeping us prisoner?'

'Oh, sure, and give the whole thing away,' Luke said, agitation in his voice. 'Rob, you need to focus. We have to get to Ralph before those giant snake things do.'

Robyn nodded miserably. 'How long ago since Ralph was seen at that mine?'

'I don't know.'

'How big is it? What if he's moved on?'

'We'll find tracks or something,' Luke insisted. 'You're good at that.'

Robyn did as Luke said, following him through the veld as he kept a lookout for any animals that might prove a threat to them. She felt so guilty for all he'd been through, she found she didn't want to argue with him. But still –

What if this is all a fever dream? she thought dismally. *What if I wake, and I'm still dying, and Luke was never here . . .*

'Hey.' Luke took her arm and steered her out the way of a thorny bush blocking her path. He passed her the bottle of water they'd taken from the Bakho cave. 'You look a million miles away. You OK?'

'Not really,' she admitted. She swigged from the bottle, then licked her dry lips. 'I guess you don't just bounce back from Gerhard's virus in a few hours.'

'You're lucky to be alive,' Luke agreed.

'So are you.' Robyn tried to focus her thoughts as she carried on walking. 'I can't believe you just rode out of Gerhard's complex on a trail bike with the injuries you had.'

'You'd have done the same,' Luke said quietly. 'Anything to survive. When the stakes are that high . . .'

'I suppose. Even so, you must have roamed for days.'

'I lost track of how long it was.' Luke led her through a stand of acacia trees. In the distance Robyn saw a dull, concrete building nestled against a hill behind a high chain-link fence. She felt a fizz of fresh enthusiasm.

'Is that the mine where Ralph was seen?'

'Yep. Come on.'

His certainty puzzled Robyn. 'How do you know?'

'I passed it the day before the Bakho found me,' Luke said impatiently. He drank from his water bottle and passed it to her. 'Now, come *on*.'

The water, and the hope of finding a clue to Ralph's whereabouts, made Robyn feel a little stronger as she kept up with Luke. Finally, she'd be back with her brother and the three of them could start looking for her dad and Xai, Grant and Niko. There had to be something they could do . . .

The sun was sinking. The mine workings behind the fence shimmered in a heat haze. Robyn began to worry that it was a mirage. As they drew closer, she noticed a small split in the fence near ground level. 'We can get in there,' she suggested.

'The place is deserted,' said Luke. 'Let's try the main gate. It's probably not even locked, and it's where Ralph would've made for, I bet.'

Robyn was about to follow when she heard something. A deep, sinister hissing. She recognised it at once. 'Oh, no.' She grabbed Luke's arm. 'Come on! That gap in the fence, we've got to try it!'

'Why?' Luke protested.

A second later, he had his answer. A gargantuan serpent slid out from the overgrown bushes near the fence.

A titanoboa.

It was dark green, its scales shining iridescent in the sinking sunlight. Its red eyes flashed as its mouth opened to reveal ivory fangs. Its bulk rippled revoltingly as it covered the ground between them.

'No!' Luke froze. 'No, please . . .'

'Run!' Robyn tried to drag Luke away, but he'd fallen to his knees in terror. 'Luke, if you don't come now –'

'Make it stop!' Luke yelled up at the sky, as if shouting at God. 'Call it off, please. Not the predasaurs. Not again!'

'Luke?' Robyn pulled on his arm harder. 'Please. I won't leave you –'

The snake was undulating towards them, jaws shaking, almost like it was laughing.

Luke threw back his head and bellowed again. 'I brought her to you! Did what you asked! Please . . .'

Robyn stared, shaken. 'What?'

The monstrous serpent reared up, a string of saliva hanging from its mouth, the scaly patterns on its side dancing as its giant body circled like a noose around them, ready to close in.

'Please.' Luke was sobbing now. '*Gerhard, please!*'

The serpent froze, its tongue flicking in and out. But Robyn hardly noticed. She went on staring at Luke, feeling sick. 'Gerhard?'

'That's right, Robyn. Me.'

Robyn spun around at the sound of the hateful voice. Gerhard stood behind the fence, holding a tablet in one hand, a smirk on his pale face. Robyn tried to run, but

Gerhard tapped on the tablet's screen, and the titanoboa lunged forward to cut off her bid for escape.

'Thank you, Luke,' Gerhard said approvingly. 'Thank you for bringing her to me. Now I have two little Ballantynes – and power over their father.'

'You never were his prisoner, were you, Luke?' Robyn breathed. 'You never did escape. Why would you help *him*?'

'If I didn't, he said my mum and dad would be killed.' Luke looked down at the ground, the words spilling from him. 'He brought me here and told me to let the Bakho catch me. He reckoned, cos of Xai, that you might try to reach them, so he put me there to watch out for you all.'

'My spy in the camp,' Gerhard agreed happily. 'I had no idea the Bakho were so advanced. Luke tells me that old witch doctor's natural medicines have had quite the therapeutic effect . . .'

Robyn glared at Luke as everything fell into place. 'It wasn't Senosi talking to Gerhard. It was you.'

'You have a gift for stating the obvious, my dear,' Gerhard said softly. 'Now, Luke. What about the elders' miracle botanical herb cures, hmm? Did you bring the plant samples, as instructed?'

Luke lowered his head.

Gerhard coldly stabbed a finger against the tablet's screen and the titanoboa lowered its head too. 'You did bring them, didn't you, Luke?'

Robyn could see the monster snake's jaws twitching, and the raw hunger in its red eyes. She didn't need to be a snake charmer to know the titanoboa was longing to bite Luke, its predator instincts barely held in check by the implants that had been inserted into its body. She was both breathlessly scared and sorry for the creature: a wild, incredible beast conjured from ancient times just to be tamed by a twisted master.

'I . . . I couldn't find them.' Luke was sobbing quietly, his eyes tightly shut. 'Please, Mr Gerhard. I tried, but Senosi, he keeps the stuff locked up. Robyn – you know about the cure, right?'

'No,' she snapped.

'But they gave it to you –'

'I wasn't conscious at the time!' Robyn broke across him. 'I was dying!'

'That's cute,' said Gerhard. 'Your use of the past tense, I mean. *Was* dying . . .' He gave a chuckle that chilled Robyn to the bone, but she refused to let him see her reaction to his scare tactics, and kept her attention squarely on Luke.

'See what you've done?' she hissed coldly. 'You would've been safe with the Bakho! They'd have helped us.'

'Oh, they'll be helping all right.' Gerhard nodded slowly. 'Now, come inside. You want to catch up with your brother, don't you?'

'So he *is* here?' Robyn hugged herself. 'He's all right?'

'He's alive.'

'So what do you want with us now?'

'Oh, Robyn, you know me. I'm out for blood.' Gerhard grinned nastily and swiped his finger across the screen. '*Ballantyne* blood.'

As if released from an invisible clamp, the titanoboa twisted into life again, circling around Robyn and Luke and hissing angrily. Luke scrambled up. Robyn found herself clinging to him, despite what he'd done. He looked so wretched. For all her talk of betrayal, to save her dad or Ralph – or herself – would she have defied Gerhard?

The rippling, scaly bulk of the beast made a horrible rasping sound as it stirred the dry soil, shepherding Robyn and Luke away.

Gerhard watched them go. The serpent ought to lead them to the main doors of the facility without incident, but he knew that one of his team would be monitoring its progress by camera drone, ready to intercede if necessary. To think he'd planned to kill the Ballantyne girl, not suspecting her true value. *Always learning*, he thought happily, swiping on the tablet to call Julius's private hotline.

The phone was answered swiftly. 'Well?' Mbato demanded.

'The boy brought me Ballantyne's daughter,' Gerhard said calmly, 'but not the wild extracts I need to study.'

Mbato's tone was stony. 'I told you he was unreliable. Still, if the girl's caught the virus and recovered, surely you can compare her blood against her brother's and see what antibodies can be harvested?'

'Obviously,' Gerhard said through gritted teeth. 'But we need to understand the other part of the equation. We need the drugs they used on her.'

Mbato paused. 'So, what do you propose?'

'Your old poacher friends have not yet secured Ballantyne or the rest,' said Gerhard. 'Perhaps they can better earn their fee on a side-mission . . .'

24

With Moth and Xai, Grant followed Yonker along a narrow, almost invisible path up the overgrown mountain slope. Roland had stayed behind in the jeep to take care of Niko, and Grant wondered if he should've stayed too. But Niko was insistent – she wanted everyone else as far from her as possible, so she didn't infect them. Grant couldn't help wondering how much longer it would take before the infection tightened its deadly hold on her.

The path led to the secret cache of weapons – and, according to Moth, it was a starting point for a likely Bakho 'place of hiding'. The tension and sense of urgency was palpable as they pushed themselves faster and harder over the difficult terrain. Grant gazed down thirstily at a large pool of floodwater in the plain beside the mountainside, where a herd of skittish zebras huddled.

'I remember this place,' Xai said quietly. 'I spent time in these mountains as a child when my parents visited family.'

'Were your parents forced to leave?' Moth asked.

'No. They simply believed it was best for me,' Xai said.

'They tired of the persecution. Of having so little say in their own fates.' He shrugged. 'I used to wander around everywhere, sticking my nose into things. The local folks were happy to teach me some skills.'

'So you were an outsider too,' Moth said, wondering.

'If you love and give to these lands,' said Xai, 'you will always be a part of them.'

Just then Yonker came to an abrupt stop. 'I think I hear . . .'

The murmur of rotor blades swelled over the treetops.

'They're still searching,' Grant murmured.

Xai grabbed Yonker by the shoulder. 'How far now to your weapons?'

'Another twenty minutes, at least,' Yonker said. 'This track's exit point is coming up soon, then it's harder going through the brush.'

'We need to find cover,' Grant said.

'Look.' Moth pointed to the helicopter, which rose into sight over the trees like a malevolent horsefly. Lights shining, it hovered over the summit of the rocky outcrop.

Grant saw black-clad figures drop from it, four of them, silhouetted in the copter's lights. For a moment he thought they had fallen and were plunging to their doom. But no; they were rappelling down ropes, dropping out of sight.

'What are they doing?' Yonker whispered. 'There's nothing there.'

'That's one of the sites on Moth's map,' said Grant. 'Maybe they know –'

'What Moth guessed already,' Xai agreed, gripping his

assault rifle. 'Yonker, we have to move.'

Yonker pulled a face. 'Before we've got the weapons? Those troops will be armed.'

'We'll scout around, get the lie of the land,' Xai insisted. 'We must do what we can to help the tribe.'

'We could use their help with Niko too,' Grant agreed.

'And if we can take any of Mbato's troops prisoner, we might learn something that'll help us. All right.' Yonker pulled a flashlight from his pocket. 'Moth, take Grant and get the weapons – bring them back here and wait for us. Any sign of trouble, ditch them and run.' Yonker placed a hand on Moth's shoulder and touched his forehead to hers. 'Who's my girl, eh?'

'Me,' said Moth, and embraced him, then turned and hurried away into the foliage.

Xai caught Grant's hand as he made to follow her, then shook it. 'Till we meet again, my young friend.'

Grant bit his lip and nodded. He had the awful feeling that meeting might never happen.

The helicopter had dropped off all its occupants, and now it rose higher into the air, turning. Soon it would be overhead.

'Move!' With a hearty shove, Yonker propelled Grant after Moth.

Grant followed the sound of her progress through the vegetation and the dancing light of her torch beam. Even in the gloom he could see her lithe, nimble figure darting like a dragonfly into every gap in the undergrowth and muddy hollow. Well, he was taller but just as determined so, ignoring the scratches of thorns and the bruises of branches, he fought his way through a landscape set on keeping its secrets. The hard thrust of rotors could be heard again, carrying through the leaf canopy. He kept thinking of Roland and Niko, sitting targets in the jeep, and prayed the copter wouldn't spot them.

Moth came to a sudden stop, playing the torch beam around a tiny clearing. She gave a quiet hiss of triumph as she located an old scarf, covered in mud to disguise it as an old vine, tied around a branch. She pushed the base of the torch into the muddy ground like a lamp, and began to unwind the material. 'Help me to pull on it.'

Grant stood beside her and caught hold of the scarf. 'What do you think the soldiers are doing? Why would mercenaries attack a small tribe?'

'I don't know.' She heaved on the strip of fabric, and Grant pulled too. With a rattle, a panel of bamboo and brushes woven together with weeds pulled clear to reveal a long green metal box with a rusting lid, hidden in a hollow. Grant helped Moth manhandle it out. There was a combination padlock, and Moth quickly opened it.

Inside were several black plastic cases, neatly packed with insulated foam.

'Rifles, handguns, ammo, grenades. All there.' Moth smiled sadly. 'Dad calls it his insurance. He said he hoped he'd never have to use it.'

Grant picked up a small case with a strap, designed to be worn around the neck. He flipped open the catch and lifted the lid. Inside he found a set of high-powered binoculars.

In a pouch in the case was a flashlight. He turned it on and almost blinded himself. 'Whoa. Stronger than I thought.'

'I know I am.' Moth slammed the lid, smirking. 'But you've still got to help me carry this thing.'

Grant raised an eyebrow. 'Was that you making a joke?' Moth's smirk turned into a full-on grin.

'We need to get back to the others,' Grant said. 'Fast.'

The path should've been easier to navigate on the return journey, but it was made a hundred times harder by the heavy box. Grant's muscles ached and his breath scraped against his dry throat. His clothes were soaked with sweat and his broken finger, though mostly healed, soon throbbed, as if sharp teeth were gnawing at his joints.

Suddenly, there was a crash behind him. Moth had dropped the case. Then she took Grant down in a rough tackle. He fell flat on his face. 'What the hell . . . ?'

'Switch off your torch,' Moth hissed, as she did the same. They clung together, gasping for breath. Grant realised how close they were to the track when he heard the sound of running footsteps approaching.

'Soldiers,' Moth hissed. 'I thought I saw their torchlight.'

Four men ran past their hiding place, each weighed down with heavy packs and bags. There was a sound of breaking glass, and someone swore.

'Leave it!' came a low voice. 'We've got enough of their bloody plant life to start our own garden centre.'

The men started to run again, and soon the soldiers passed out of earshot.

Grant pulled away from Moth and played his own torch

around the track. He saw a glass jar smashed open on a rock. Inside were narrow, fibrous leaves in the remains of some unknown solution. From the metallic scent, it wasn't just water. Grant wiped his hands.

'The soldiers said *their plant life* . . .' he said. 'Whatever this stuff is, did Mbato's men steal it from the Bakho?'

'Makes sense. But what else did they do?' Moth's face was taut with worry. 'We need to find Dad and Xai.'

'No, wait.' Grant shook his head. 'Those soldiers must be heading for a rendezvous point to be picked up. If they keep going that way, they're going to run smack into Roland and Niko. Is there any way we can get to the jeep first and warn them?'

'The soldiers will most likely stick to the main path,' Moth said. 'If we cut down the escarpment, we might just get there first.' She opened the metal box, pulled out an assault rifle and pushed it into Grant's arms. 'Roland might need this.'

'So might we,' Grant said grimly, slotting a loaded clip into the AK-47. 'No one's come running after those soldiers. Not your dad, not Xai, not the San. What happened up there?'

'Maybe Dad and Xai drove off the soldiers,' said Moth. 'I'll take you to your people – then I'll come back looking for mine.'

Moth led the way, and Grant followed close behind. He was uneasy carrying the assault rifle, and kept checking that the safety was on. He knew that guns could only escalate the situation; if he came face to face with a combat-trained soldier, the AK-47 might prompt them to shoot first and ask questions later. But Roland was a trained soldier with the experience and skill to enforce his will on a combat situation. By delivering the weapon, Grant was empowering him to save Niko's life.

That was the hope he clung to.

He and Moth moved quickly and quietly through the denser parts of the forest, fingers over the ends of their torches to smother some of the light. Grant kept thinking he heard engines growling, hoarse shouts, but if he paused for a moment he could hear nothing.

Just your imagination, he told himself. It was like a nightmare, running all the time but never reaching the end of the chase, following the dizzying beam of Moth's torchlight through the crowded forest. Time and again he bruised himself on low branches. Thorns hooked on his sweat-soaked shirt, and he grunted as he forced himself on.

'Roland and Niko should be just the other side of that scrub mopane.' Moth's grin was as bright as the moonlight. 'We've done it! And we must have reached them ahead of those soldiers . . .'

But when Moth reached the edge of the stunted trees, whose leaves and branches had been gnawed away by hungry elephants, she stopped. Joining her, Grant swore.

The jeep had gone.

'What the hell happened?' Grant muttered, shining his torch around, praying that he wouldn't find any sign of Roland and Niko's bodies.

Moth was focusing on the tracks left behind in the shallow soil. 'Looks like the jeep was driven away.'

'Roland might have seen the soldiers coming and moved it somewhere safer,' said Grant. He hoped that wasn't just wishful thinking.

'There are signs of a scuffle in the soil,' Moth informed him, playing the torch around towards the treeline. 'And boot prints.'

'Tyre tracks too,' Grant noted. 'But they're even. No wheelspins or mud churned up to show a quick getaway.'

'Dragon One, respond.' A voice carried wire-sharp through the darkness.

Grant pulled Moth down to the ground, out of sight.

'Dragon One, what happened? Where are you?'

'Dragon's a call sign,' Moth whispered. 'That's a soldier. Close.'

Grant gripped his rifle. 'Let's check it out.'

Stealthy as cats, he and Moth moved through the leafy darkness. The voice of the soldier was like a homing signal for them, drawing them in.

And others too.

Bright headlights beamed on through the trees ahead of them. The soldier, silhouetted now, barely twenty metres away, opened fire. Grant shielded his eyes and ducked with Moth behind the nearest tree. As his vision adjusted he saw a dark figure detach itself from the shadows and shoot the soldier in the back of the neck. Grant flinched at the callous violence. As the soldier fell, the figure removed their well-filled pack then straightened. Grant caught a glint of gold in a satisfied smile.

Rontane, he realised.

The soldier clearly hadn't been able to get hold of the rest of his unit over the radio, and it wasn't hard to guess why. The poachers were fighting back: literally stealing the advantage from Mbato's soldiers by picking them off, one by one. Roland had tricked the two camps into aggression at Yonker's place, and now the die was cast. Rontane crossed to the headlights.

'Looks like Dad's jeep,' Moth murmured.

Grant closed his eyes. 'Which means that Abrafo and his gang have got Roland and Niko.'

25

Ralph felt groggy and cold. Pain was arrowing through his back and his throat was parched. Gerhard's pet scientists had taken so much blood that he'd lost consciousness. When he'd woken again, the first thing he was aware of was the stench of preservatives and disinfectant in the freezing air, overlying the faint scent of rot. He recognised the smell from the animal pens at Crocodile Lodge – the only part of home that Ralph hadn't missed these last weeks on the run.

He was lying on a metal slab, like a corpse. A dim light shone through high, dusty windows. *So not all the complex is underground*, he thought. From the outside the place must look like just another old mine building. Inside, however, the feel was more modern and clinical. Steel benches and trolley tables were stacked in one corner. Drainage channels ran across the floor. A sheet covered a lumpy shape on one of the benches like a shroud, and a large, heavy-duty incinerator dominated one wall, its aluminium chimney stretching up through the ceiling. *That's why we're above ground here,*

Ralph realised. *So the smoke and ash from whatever they burn have somewhere to go.*

He had been dumped in a mortuary for animals. Ready, he guessed, for the next round of tests.

But there was another figure in the room, scarred and pale, slumped against the heavy, aluminium cold-room door. Ralph sat up sharp in shock. 'Luke! What's happening? Why are you here?'

Luke got up stiffly from the floor, picked up a ceramic jug and poured liquid into a beaker. 'A mortuary's the best place for me, huh?'

Ralph thought he must be dreaming. Wild thoughts stabbed at his brain. *They must've put Luke in here cos he was dead. Luke's back as a zombie!*

'Stay away,' Ralph warned him, visions from *Resident Evil* flashing through his mind.

Luke frowned. 'I figured you could use a glass of water.'

'I mean it!'

'Come on, get your crap together,' Luke said sharply, pushing the beaker into Ralph's hands. 'You're not dreaming. I'm not a nightmare. Gerhard saved me from those monster hyenas cos he wanted to use me . . . and that's just what he's done.'

Ralph pushed aside the mental visions of zombies and swigged the water. 'What do you mean?'

'I'm sorry.' Luke looked down at the floor, ashamed. 'I led Robyn here.'

Anger hardened like steel through Ralph's body. 'You did what?'

'The Bakho were looking after her. She was sick, but they helped heal her, and now Gerhard's got her. He wants to see how she survived the virus.'

'I thought it was her leg that was bad.' Ralph scowled and shook his head. 'How's Gerhard going to find out how she survived? By taking her apart, cell by cell?'

'I don't know.' Luke's watery eyes showed his contrition. 'I didn't want to bring Robyn here, dude, but Gerhard threatened my family.'

'I kind of know the feeling,' Ralph shot back.

'You know what, Ralph? Snark all you want, but where's that gonna get you?' Luke looked at him. 'If we work together, maybe we can get out of here and help Robyn.'

You've helped her enough, Ralph wanted to say, but he bit his tongue. Begrudgingly, he had to admit that Luke was right; staying angry would do nothing to help the situation. 'I guess Gerhard doesn't just want us for our blood. He'll be using us as bait for Dad.'

'Right,' Luke agreed. 'So, we have to get out of here and help her.'

'Until Gerhard snaps his fingers and you change sides again?'

Luke ignored him and knocked on the metal door. 'This thing is locked from the outside. No way out from in here, so . . . the only chance we have to get out is –'

'If we make someone open it for us,' Ralph concluded. 'Agreed, but how?'

'It's mostly doctors and vets and stuff here, right? Not rangers, like Gerhard's reserve. There's only Abi – and she's injured.' Luke shrugged. 'All we need is for them to open the door . . .'

'And then maybe we can surprise them. Force our way out.' Ralph frowned. 'But even if we manage to get outside, there are giant mega-snakes guarding the fence. Those things are the reason Gerhard doesn't need a ton of guards.'

Luke shuddered, looking pale. 'Jeez, I hate snakes. Even regular ones. That thing I saw outside . . . it was terrifying.'

Try finding yourself half inside one, thought Ralph. 'It's how Gerhard controls them from his tablet that freaks me out. How does he do it?'

Luke raised his eyebrows and pondered. 'He must use an AI chip hardwired into the snakes' brains, like a secondary brain, ready to suppress and correct the snake's natural behaviour whenever it's activated.'

Ralph was impressed. 'How'd you know that?'

'My dad runs the biggest security tech business in South Africa,' Luke reminded him. 'What Gerhard's done is genius, obvs, but it's basically the same as using your smartphone to control the lights and the thermostat in your home. Only the software and the sensors must be a million times more complicated.'

'Making a snake into a living robot . . .' Ralph had to marvel at the technology. 'What does that take?'

'A brain's just another computer, right?' Luke said. 'But it uses chemical signals as well as electrical ones. So if Gerhard's controlling it, his computer chip must be hacking those signals, yeah?'

'But a brain's got millions of neurons to do its thinking,' Ralph argued, channelling his biology teacher. 'How does Gerhard's chip bypass that?'

'It must have online connectivity. It'll be linked to some big data analysis,' Luke said. 'Gerhard's working those snakes from a tablet, but that can't have the computing power he'd need . . .' He clicked his fingers. 'It's like remote desktop gaming. There must be a data centre here, packed full of servers that do all the processing – crunching all the numbers you need to simulate those neuron things.'

Ralph felt optimism rise falteringly inside him. 'If you're right, then we've got two options,' Ralph said. 'We can steal Gerhard's tablet and try to control the mega-snakes ourselves . . .'

'Oh yeah, I can totally see him handing that over,' Luke said drily. 'And I can see us working it first time without a hitch while being chased by literally everyone.'

'Then we've got one option,' Ralph said. 'Find Gerhard's data centre and trash it – so then no one can control the mega-snakes.'

Luke looked at him. 'So they'll still want to catch and kill us, but they won't have an off switch.'

'At least we might stand a chance,' Ralph said fiercely. 'At least we wouldn't be the only ones the snakes would be after. But we're gonna stand no chance at all if we can't get out of this mortuary . . .' He tailed off. He had heard something. A low note, slowly stealing into the landscape outside. 'Engine noise,' Ralph said. 'Someone's coming.'

Luke heard the sound and looked up at the high window.

'If we push this table over and stick a chair on it . . . I can't climb so well any more, but I guess you can.'

Ralph felt a pang of sympathy, and guilt that he'd come through Gerhard's games a little better than Luke. So far, at least. Luke held the chair steady while Ralph climbed up and peered out through the glass. He saw a jeep driving towards the canteen building. With a shiver, he saw that Rontane was in the driver's seat. Beside her was a heavy-set man he didn't recognise. But when the jeep pulled up just outside the main doors, he saw who was in the back of the jeep, guarded by two more poachers. His heart stuttered.

It was Roland Ballantyne.

He was dragged out, semi-conscious, his hands cuffed behind his back, leaving Niko slumped on the back seat.

'Dad,' Ralph whispered.

'No way!' Luke swore. 'Is he coming to the rescue?'

'No. He's a prisoner. Niko too, only she looks really sick.' As Ralph watched, two people came outside, clothed head to toe in hazard suits, looking like astronauts on a lunar surface, carrying a stretcher. They swiftly transferred Niko onto it and vanished inside as quickly as they'd appeared. Ralph bit his lip as he saw his dad try to bolt from his captors. But the man in the front was surprisingly fast. He tripped Roland so he fell face-first in the dust. Rontane kicked him in the ribs before the two poachers dragged him to his feet.

Straining to hear over his racing heart, Ralph caught his dad's words. 'Where're they taking her, Abrafo?'

'You'll see,' the man said.

'Abrafo.' Ralph felt dread whisper along his spine as his dad was forced inside the building.

'Who's Abrafo?' Luke asked.

'Another worst nightmare. Things are kicking off,' Ralph said, looking down at Luke. 'We've got to get out of here and find Dad and Niko and Robyn. Somehow, we've just got to!'

Grant woke to the sound of heavy footsteps crashing through the undergrowth. Light spilled through the cracks in the rotten tree trunk he lay in, and he cursed himself for falling asleep. Where was Moth? She was meant to be keeping guard. The rifle was still clasped to his chest but there was no way he could use it here even if he'd wanted to. The steps got closer.

'It's all right.' Moth sounded excited. 'Come out.'

'Where'd you go?'

'I heard a noise,' she said, as Grant emerged from inside the log, 'and so I left you while I went to see . . .'

'And she found us!' Yonker burst into the clearing like a bear chasing a picnic basket. 'We're all right, boy! Skin of our teeth, though, eh? Quite the *jollie patrollie*.'

'I am seriously glad to see you,' said Grant. 'We were going to look for you at dawn, but it was too risky in the dark with soldiers and poachers and –'

'Moth told us what happened,' said Yonker. 'I'm sorry we left you hanging. Things got serious at Bakho Mountain.'

Grant frowned. 'Then . . . you managed to find the place?'

'Your friend called it Bakho Mountain. We call it home.'

Another man entered the clearing, dressed in a scorched, crumpled patchwork of brightly coloured prints and leathers. 'Forgive my appearance. I am Senosi, a leader among my people.' He was carrying a cracked glass case with some withered-looking leaves inside. 'Those soldiers – men sent by Mbato – rappelled into our land to steal and kill.'

'We cut a path through in time to help,' Xai said. 'But some of them got away.'

'Reckon the poachers took care of them,' Grant said. 'Permanently.'

'Ten of my brothers and sisters have been murdered,' Senosi said. 'So much violence, inflicted solely so they could steal all supplies of a drug we discovered. A drug that could change the course of the new pandemic. And half of the supplies they took are ruined, discarded on the ground.'

Moth blinked. 'Plant cures? I had heard that the Bakho use special medicines the West doesn't have,' she said. 'The West always thinks it's fine to take from . . . from you.'

Senosi looked at Moth intently, sizing her up. Then he spoke slowly in Bakho.

Moth looked shocked, but she found her voice and managed to say something back.

'I disagree,' Senosi said with a smile. 'I think you speak our dialect very well.'

Yonker nodded, pride in his eyes. 'Doesn't she just. And I never knew.'

'Well, events like last night's make fast learners of us all,' Senosi declared.

'Clearly we have a common enemy, Senosi,' said Xai,

getting them back on track. 'We both need precious things returned to us.'

'No doubt they were taken to Gerhard's lab complex at the old mine,' said Senosi. 'Our trackers have already followed Robyn and Luke there . . .'

'Luke?' Grant reacted as if he'd been struck. 'Luke van Rok?'

Senosi nodded.

'But Luke's dead! We heard it happen . . . we heard him screaming for help!'

'Gerhard called off his predasaurs and let him live. Must've decided Luke was worth more to him alive,' said Xai.

Grant couldn't believe what he was hearing. 'We need to get to this old mine,' he said. 'If Gerhard's there, that's got to be where Abrafo would take Roland and Niko and the Bakho medicines.'

'He holds everything that Gerhard and Mbato want,' Xai agreed. 'Now he's taken care of the mercs, he can pretty much name his price.'

'I bet Mbato's already on his way,' said Grant. 'So, what do we do? Take the weapons and hit Gerhard's base?'

'I don't see that we have a choice,' said Yonker. 'Senosi, you must have warriors in the tribe, right?'

Senosi looked unhappy. 'We have already lost so many today . . .'

'But we have to fight,' Moth said solemnly. 'Don't we?'

26

Robyn strained against the handcuffs that attached her to the head of the stainless-steel trolley table, though she knew it was hopeless. She was chafing her wrists raw and there was no chance of the cuffs giving – particularly since she'd had so much blood taken by Gerhard's medical staff, plus the samples that Senosi had taken. If only she was back there, safe. If only Ralph had found his way there too!

A doctor in a mask and scrubs was labelling the latest phial of her blood. 'You might as well stop trying to fight the table and just lie on it.'

Robyn let her burning arms hang limp and closed her eyes. Gerhard had taken her to an anteroom beside a well-equipped operating theatre, and she'd noted from the pens in the recovery area that it was designed for large animals, not people. The medics she'd met might well have been veterinary technicians by trade; they'd certainly treated her like an animal, talking about her as if she wasn't able to hear or understand, prodding her awake when she fell asleep, squirting water down her throat with a tube to keep her hydrated. It was perhaps the worst nightmare she'd had to endure, and she kept thinking: *How much more of this can I take?*

'Does it make you feel better about what you're doing here?' she hissed. 'Is it easier if you pretend that I'm an animal for testing, not a fifteen-year-old girl your boss has kidnapped?'

'You're a dangerous fugitive, we're told,' one of the masked medics said, and Robyn recognised the voice at once. The 'medic' pulled down her mask. It was Abi.

Robyn recovered from her surprise. 'You're a doctor now? I thought you were in security.'

'I trained as a field medic in the army,' she said. 'Shrinker's work paid better.'

'Until it nearly killed you.' Robyn glared at her. 'I saved your life.'

'If I don't do what Gerhard tells me – even mopping the floors – I'm dead,' Abi said quietly. 'Dead as your whole family's going to wind up.'

Robyn swallowed hard. 'Ralph . . . he's not . . .'

'Oh, for now, he's peachy. Thanks to him, we finally got a hold of your phone. The one with the video of Mbato leading the hunting party after the sarcosuchus.'

Robyn felt sick but tried to keep her face neutral. The handset was dead after so long without charging, but some nights, knowing that the precious evidence against their president was buried safely inside that electronic tomb was the only thing that kept her going. It offered some small hope that they would bring Mbato's crimes to light and him to justice, whatever spin the president tried to put on it.

'Gerhard dumped the handset in acid,' Abi said simply.

'That . . . that doesn't matter.' Robyn closed her eyes. 'We uploaded it to the cloud straight after taking it –'

'With no signal? Give it up, Robyn,' Abi said. 'In any case, you'd need something way more impressive than a shaky video to bring down the president and his number-one donor.' She sounded almost disappointed.

Robyn was about to tell Abi to go to hell when a haunting, high-pitched cry cut the air like a knife. Robyn realised it was coming from a pen in the next room; an animal had woken in distress. 'What animal is that?'

'Woolly rhino,' Abi said, turning back to the phial of blood and placing it in a sterile envelope.

'What's wrong with it?' Robyn demanded, as grunting sobs carried into the operating room. 'It sounds like it's in pain.'

'It probably is.'

'Then give it something that will help!'

'Can't,' said Abi dully. 'Pain and stress make them better predasaurs.'

'Do you hear yourself?' Robyn hissed, her whisper as icy as the sterile air. Abi limped away with her blood sample. Robyn raised her voice: 'Do you see what you've become? It's one thing to beat up people, but helpless animals . . .'

It was no use. Abi's face was turned away as she left, closing the door quietly behind her.

Robyn relaxed her arms and pulled away from the trolley as far as she could to try to see the woolly rhino in the next room. A tingle ran through her as she made eye contact with a beast that hadn't walked the planet for 50,000 years. Although young, it was already as big as a sideboard. Its eyes were bloodshot, but albino pink rather than red; it didn't seem as crazed and angry as the other predasaurs she'd seen, either, despite whatever Gerhard was doing to it.

The beast was fidgeting, twitching, snorting, banging its stubby horn against the bars of its cage.

'It's all right,' she whispered. 'You'll get through this . . .' Robyn's attempts to reach out to Gerhard's creations had always crashed and burned. *But if it knows pain*, she reasoned, *perhaps it can sense kindness*. She calmed her breathing and maintained eye contact, willing the young animal to trust her. It was difficult over a distance, but she ignored her own pain and focused on trying to soothe the juvenile. Slowly, the young rhino began to stop fidgeting. It held eye contact with her. Still it snorted, but not so loudly. Robyn felt a thrill stir in her soul at the unexpected connection.

But then the door behind her was flung open. Robyn gasped and jolted. The woolly rhino squealed in alarm and began to whine. When she saw who had entered, Robyn wanted to do the same.

Gerhard stood in the doorframe. Rontane hovered just behind him, loaded up with jars of green fluid that Robyn thought she'd seen before in Senosi's lab. Next to them a dark window in the wall suddenly flickered with brightness – an observation window for the operating theatre situated next door. Two people in PPE were fussing over someone on a table –

'Niko?' Robyn breathed.

'Oh. You've spoiled the surprise now,' Gerhard said wryly. 'Your father's girlfriend is at death's door, it seems. She has the virus.'

'How . . . convenient for you,' Robyn said, trying to stay cool. 'You can test out your cure on her.'

'One doesn't synthesise a vaccine overnight,' Gerhard informed her. 'But your blood differs from your brother's in several small, but important, ways as a result of your infection – and subsequent treatment. A blood transfusion from you is worth a try.'

Robyn felt a prickle of hope stir inside her. 'You think a direct transfusion could help Niko?'

'I know your father has a natural immunity to Ebola. I suspect that the Bakho plant cure has boosted the antiviral proteins in your blood – type I interferons, which limit the way the virus replicates. Or perhaps it's certain immune cells – memory T-cells that formed during your infections – that are boosted by the plants. So much to learn, eh, my dear? And poor Niko is dying to find out . . .' He tipped his head to one side and smiled. 'The problem is, we've taken so much blood out of you already. So, if you do give her a transfusion, you could die.'

Robyn refused to show her fear. 'How do you even know that my blood's compatible with Niko's?'

'Because your daddy told me . . .' Gerhard's lips pulled back in a rictus grin. 'In the end.'

'Dad!' Robyn cried as Roland Ballantyne was pushed in through the door by a stocky, bearded man.

'Robyn,' Roland said hoarsely, eyes bright in his bloodied face. 'Are you all right?'

The man jammed a gun to his jaw. 'Quit shooting your mouth off. Or it happens for real.'

'You have no say in what happens to me,' Roland said coldly, with a glance at Gerhard. 'Or is Angel Abrafo running the show now?'

'Abrafo?' Robyn stared, askance. So this was the man she'd heard tales of for so long. The man with so much blood on his hands, and nothing in his eyes but money.

'Mr Abrafo is for Mbato to deal with,' Gerhard said airily. 'And indeed, Mr Ballantyne is right to be concerned. If we don't attempt a transfusion, Niko will surely die. But if we do, he could lose Robyn as well. It's a dilemma, for sure.'

'No dilemma,' Robyn said shakily. 'I'm strong enough.'

Roland looked at her. 'No one has the right to ask you to do this, Robyn –'

'And no one has the right to stop me.' She'd made up her mind. Niko had fought with them, saved them, endured every hardship with them. And her dad loved Niko. Robyn would save her if she could.

'If you're through with the nauseating platitudes, we have a medical team itching to get going here.' Gerhard put a hand on Robyn's shoulder. 'The work we do here could help us to save millions.'

'And help you to make *billions*,' Roland said, disgusted.

212

'You'll be able to name your price for a vaccine against a virus you unleashed yourself.'

'Yes, I will, won't I? All thanks to you Ballantynes.' Gerhard gave a happy little sigh. 'That deserves a reward, doesn't it? Tell you what. I'll keep Mbato's hands off you for just a while longer.'

'Hold on, *Mr* Gerhard,' Rontane drawled. 'We just took out a squad of mercs. We're not hanging around this freak house for their mates to follow up in that helicopter.'

'We kept our side of the contract,' Abrafo agreed. 'Now Mbato needs to call off his dogs and pay us.'

'Oh, he'll pay all right,' Roland muttered.

Gerhard nodded to the operating room, where the medical technicians were setting up IV bags and drips around Niko. 'He might pay less for her dead than alive.'

'You've got a nerve. If this virus really *is* yours, you should be paying extra – compensation for Chikondi's death.' Rontane raised one of the jars of dirty green water, ready to shatter it on the ground. 'You should know: give less, get less.'

'So, get on to Mbato,' said Abrafo threateningly. 'Right now.'

Gerhard gave them an icy look before resuming his urbane manner. 'I understand,' he purred. 'You beat the competition to the kill like true apex predators. I commend you for that. But Mbato invested in those mercenaries –'

'I'm happy to discuss that with him.' Abrafo smiled mirthlessly. 'So, get him on the line.'

'What about Niko?' Robyn said. 'While you're gloating with the president, she's going downhill with every breath.'

'The medics are assessing Ms Haart's baseline vital signs,' Gerhard said, pulling out his phone. 'And you must be prepped also, my dear. We have a few minutes yet.'

Robyn looked at her dad. She wanted to cry, seeing his face so bruised and bloodied.

'I'm OK,' he mouthed to her.

'Me too,' she mouthed back.

The door opened and Abi came back in, leaning heavily on her makeshift crutch. 'You called me, sir?'

'About time,' Gerhard snapped, tapping on his phone. 'Get Miss Ballantyne ready for direct donor transfusion.'

Abi shifted uncomfortably. 'A reminder, sir, that I'm out of practice with –'

'No excuses,' Gerhard snapped. 'You're only assisting with the procedure. This is an ideal opportunity to see the effects of the girl's blood in an active intervention. If Ms Haart makes a full or partial recovery, we'll know that our miracle cure is on the right track.' He smiled at Robyn. 'And you'll know you're performing an invaluable service for Mbato by keeping your could've-been-step-mummy alive to face justice . . .'

Robyn looked away. But when she saw Abi sorting through large syringes and cannulas from a box of veterinary supplies, she wished she hadn't.

'Ah!' said Gerhard into his phone. 'Julius? How's the pandemic playing out?'

Abrafo signalled with the gun for Gerhard to put the call on speakerphone so he could hear. It seemed he didn't trust Gerhard either.

'The virus is spreading fast.' Mbato's voice sounded through the room. 'Compared to Covid, there are more cases that are asymptomatic, but those who get it are dying fast. We could be looking at the biggest contagion since the Black Death.'

Robyn felt a chill run through her. To know that she might hold the key to helping save lives on such a scale – and that she might die in the process . . . It felt overwhelming.

'Now, you promised me news, Gerhard. We've lost contact with most of Dragon squad. What's happened?'

'They're casualties of war.' Abrafo left his sidekick to guard Roland while he sauntered over to Gerhard. 'But their mission was a success . . . for us.'

'Abrafo?' Mbato paused. 'I'd given up on you. Thought you'd failed me.'

'Then you are foolish . . . sir,' Abrafo said. 'Back in your army days, I paid you to turn a blind eye to my business. Now you will pay me for doing your business.'

'I already paid a good deal up front to those mercenaries.'

'We all make business decisions we come to regret.' Abrafo chuckled. 'Come through for us, or you'll regret that particular decision a great deal.'

'Very well. I'll transfer funds to the usual account, Abrafo,' Mbato said. 'With deductions in place for failing to hand over Xai and the Khumalo boy.'

Abrafo's face darkened. 'You have the Ballantynes! They're the real targets.'

'Strictly speaking,' Gerhard put in, 'it was me who successfully abducted the Ballantyne children.'

'But we got the Bakho medicines,' Rontane snarled, holding up her haul. 'If you don't want them, just say so and I'll burn the whole lot. Good luck with staying in power without your vaccine, Mr President.'

Robyn watched with dread as Abi added forceps and clips to her storage box full of medical paraphernalia, then walked towards her. The woman seemed nervous, but then Robyn supposed that a transfusion like this was hardly everyday stuff. Quietly Abi sorted through the keys on a big ring, ready to unlock Robyn's handcuffs. It had become habitual for Robyn to search any situation for a chance to escape, but she realised here that the strategy was no use. Even if she did get away, Niko would die.

'All right, Abrafo,' said Mbato after deliberating. 'We'll do business as arranged. But I want Xai and Khumalo delivered too.'

'Xai's a Bakho – maybe they've seen him and the boy?' Abrafo shrugged. 'We can round them up and kill the rest of the Bakho if you want. Blame it on Dragon squad, say they went rogue.'

'That may not be necessary. You can bet that Ballantyne's little rogue will be planning a rescue mission,' Mbato went on. 'Put Ballantyne somewhere prominent and he'll make fine bait.'

Robyn saw her dad sneer and turn his face away.

'Bait for a snake trap,' said Gerhard, a smile spreading over his face. 'Pity the drones are still on charge. A titanoboa ambush would make the most breath-taking cut-scene for *The Serpent's Lair*.'

'You're sick,' Robyn breathed as Abi undid her cuffs at last. Robyn rubbed her aching wrists. 'All of you. Sick!'

'Come on,' Abi told Robyn quietly. 'Time to go.'

'The transfusion is about to begin, Julius,' Gerhard informed him. 'A better test of the girl's remarkable blood we couldn't hope for.'

'For all our sakes,' said Mbato, 'it had better work.'

He rang off, and the woolly rhino gave a screech, as if in protest. Gerhard smiled. 'Ah. Pain and stress stimulate several adaptive hormonal responses in the animal's adrenal cortex. Perhaps its pain is finally translating into aggression. It might enjoy a stay of execution after all . . .'

One of the medics from the operating room came in and wordlessly collected Abi's box of gear for the transfusion.

'Come on,' Abi said. 'Let's get on with it.' She grabbed Robyn by the arm and pushed her towards the door.

Robyn looked back at her dad as she was hauled into the operating room. He tried to give her a reassuring smile, but it only showed her that one of his teeth had been knocked out. She reached out to him with her free hand – then the door swung closed, cutting off contact.

27

Ralph was peering out of the narrow, grubby windows in the mortuary. He could see two men hammering a metal pole into the ground, like an enormous stake, some fifty metres away. They shook the pole to make sure it was secure then walked back to the main entrance.

'What's going on out there?' Luke asked, climbing precariously up onto the chair to join him. 'See anything?'

'Someone's being brought out . . .' The words died in Ralph's throat as he realised the 'someone' was his father. The two men had hauled Roland Ballantyne outside with a chain around his ankle. Now they secured that chain to the pole.

'Why hold him outside?' Ralph muttered.

'Quarantine?' Luke suggested.

'Or as bait.' Ralph watched as the two men left. The moment they were gone, Roland started to struggle against his restraints. But he stopped when an enormous, undulating shadow came sidewinding through the dust towards him.

'Titanoboa,' Luke breathed.

The beast was blue-black, like a monstrous, flailing artery brought to horrible life. How could something so enormous move so fast? It bore down on Roland with such speed that Ralph barely had time to scream. 'Dad!'

But the writhing predasaur slithered past Roland as if he wasn't there. Ralph strained to see where it went, but his view from the window was restricted. Even so, he could hear the sinister hiss and click of its flickering tongue.

'It must be sheltering behind that outhouse,' Luke realised.

'Hiding,' Ralph agreed. 'Waiting.'

Luke frowned. 'Waiting for someone to take the bait and rescue your old man?'

'Someone like Xai. Got to be. And then the snake attacks.' Ralph jumped down from his perch and banged his fists against the cold-room door. 'Let us out of here!' They were running out of time.

'Can't see anyone rushing to do that,' Luke said dourly. 'Maybe if we pretend we're sick, someone might come and –'

'Unless they're right outside the door, how will they know? No. We need to pull something unmissable . . .' Ralph stared around the room. His eyes lingered on the large, gun-metal grey incinerator with its heavy hinged doors. 'Something like fire.'

Luke looked confused. 'Huh?'

'They burn animal corpses in that thing,' said Ralph. 'And look.' He pointed to the high ceiling. 'Sprinklers and an alarm.'

'Makes sense, in case of fire.'

'So let's start one,' said Ralph, crossing to the incinerator

219

and studying the controls. It wasn't a million miles from the model his dad used back home to convert household waste to energy for the lodge using a steam turbine. 'It'll take ages to get this thing up to a proper incinerator temperature, but we don't need that.' He switched on the machine, and there was an intense hum of power. 'Just enough to start something smouldering . . .'

Luke nodded to the bulk under the shroud. 'Whatever that is?'

Ralph crossed over to the table, braced himself, then pulled the sheet away to expose the carcass of a juvenile mammoth. He shuddered as he saw the rough incisions made in the skull, presumably to get at the control chip. *No respect for the animals they create*, Ralph thought sourly. *They just slice in and see if the latest genetic modifications have worked.* 'Guess it's not so easy to control the movement of animals with four limbs. Must be why they put snakes on guard duty.'

'We saw that one slide into place,' said Luke, pacing the room. 'But we don't have much of a view from here. There could be others.'

Ralph nodded. 'So, the sooner you take them all out, the better.'

'Me?!' Luke shook his head. 'No pressure, huh?'

'Yeah, pressure,' Ralph said, bundling up the sheet that had covered the mammoth.

'Wait a sec.' Luke crossed to a shelf and picked up a bottle. 'Look at this. Formaldehyde.' He tossed it to Ralph. 'That's flammable.'

Ralph caught it and studied the label. He grinned. 'That should get the fire going a little faster.' He tipped the fluid onto the sheet and he and Luke winced at the pungent, sharp-sour smell. Then he rolled up the sodden sheet and put one end inside the incinerator. It was already hot in there, but Ralph knew it would need to get a whole lot hotter.

'Come on,' he muttered. Nervously he climbed up to the window once more, to check on his dad. Roland Ballantyne was still chained by his ankle to the pole. The chittering hiss of titanoboas carried over the distant thrum of cicadas in the wilderness beyond the fence.

Then Ralph's guts twisted as he spied two figures inside the compound, a man and a woman, approaching cautiously. 'Oh no. People coming!'

Luke gave him a sharp look. 'Poachers? Guards?'

'They . . . look like they're from a San community. Traditional San.' Ralph took in the man's clothes, which were made from animal skins, draped in a rectangle over his shoulder and chest. The woman – or was it a girl? – wore a black cloak threaded with brightly coloured beads. Each carried a bow with a quiver full of arrows. The man held a spear for good measure.

'Get back!' Roland's yell carried faintly through the glass as he struggled against his chains. 'Not safe! It's a trap! Get back!'

'They don't have a clue what's waiting for them,' Ralph muttered.

Suddenly the fabric caught fire, all in a crackling rush.

Luke stepped back as thick, white smoke filled the air, far more quickly than Ralph had expected. His eyes stung. Luke helped to catch him as he half jumped, half stumbled from the chair, then carried him in a low stoop over to the door. It only took a few more moments for the smoke alarm to sound its piercing cry.

'Stay low now,' Luke shouted over it. 'There's no good doing all this if we're too busy choking to escape!'

'Fair,' Ralph agreed.

In the smoke-filled silence, they waited for someone to arrive.

Hooked up to a heart monitor, Robyn tried to distract herself from her predicament by staring at Niko. The woman's face was barely visible beneath the mask feeding her oxygen. *Who'd have thought that I'd ever want the same thing as Gerhard?* she thought.

Robyn looked back at how far they'd come, her and Niko. She'd hated the woman for so long, that very particular hate born from resentment and fear: resentment at Niko taking her father's attention away from her. Fear that Niko would muddy Mum's memory.

But look at all we've been through, she thought. *We've lived together in a jeep for weeks. We've been attacked, hunted, infected. Risked our lives, helped and healed each other.* She traced her fingers gently over the puckered wound in her leg that Niko had sealed with the plastic strips. *We've survived*, she thought fiercely, *whatever it took, however close to death we were.*

'And you're not stopping now,' Robyn murmured to Niko's pale, still body. 'You *will* be OK.'

'Muttering prayers?' Abi remarked, as the lead medic directed her to rinse out a syringe with saline solution. 'I'm not sure anyone's listening.'

Robyn eyed the syringe. 'What's going to happen?'

The medic looked at her. His eyes were his only features visible past his PPE. 'We'll extract your blood, 20 cc at a time, then inject it into Niko, through a cannula.'

'Doesn't sound too bad,' Robyn said cautiously.

Abi shook her head. 'If we're going to make a difference to Niko's condition, we're going to need at least one and a half litres of your blood – roughly forty per cent of your total supply.'

'But you've already taken blood from me,' Robyn said.

'Yes, and you won't have replaced it all yet.' The medic paused. 'There's a good chance you'll go into hypovolemic shock. Your heart rate will rise and your blood pressure drop. Your body will divert blood away from your limbs and intestines to your heart and brain. We'll give you oxygen, but . . .'

'Will I die?'

'Who knows?' said the medic, walking away to get more equipment. 'If you do survive, there could well be organ damage.'

Robyn swallowed hard. 'But will Niko live?'

'Who's to say? Could all be for nothing. She's a tough woman but we think there's some internal bleeding.' Abi sighed. 'The big problem is if your blood starts clotting while we're feeding it to her. And since we'll be reusing syringes, there's a risk of passing on infection unless we clean them thoroughly. It all adds time.'

'Then you'd better start, hadn't you?' Robyn said, closing her eyes.

Abi hesitated. 'Listen, Robyn . . .'

But then the medic came over. 'Syringes prepped?' he asked, and Abi nodded.

'Then you can insert the cannula.'

With a nod, Abi took Robyn's wrist and rubbed some alcohol from a swab onto it. She applied a little Vaseline to the cannula. Robyn closed her eyes, felt the cold, hard scratch of the needle –

Then a siren went off outside, piercing and shrill. Robyn jumped and gasped with pain as the cannula twisted in her wrist.

'Hold still!' Abi hissed.

'Is that the fire alarm?' Robyn cried.

There was a banging from the observation window. Gerhard's face was at the glass, grey eyes bulging as he mouthed, 'Get on with it.' Then he turned away to harangue Abrafo and Rontane.

'Here goes everything, Robyn,' said Abi. And the needle went in.

28

From the cover of trees on the far side of the mine workings, Grant crouched beside Yonker, Senosi, and the eight Bakho warriors who had been chosen for the mission. All were watching tensely as Roland Ballantyne struggled against his chains under the sun's cruel brilliance.

Grant scowled. It was just like Gerhard to humiliate his opponent but, like everyone else, he suspected there was more to this display. Roland had to be the bait in a trap of some kind.

That was why Xai and Moth had disguised themselves as tribespeople before breaching the fence. They carried the simple but effective hunting weapons of the Bakho – a bow with arrows dipped in poison made from the larvae of leaf beetles, and a spear dipped in the same. If Gerhard or his goons were watching, they would no doubt be sniggering at the sight of two natives unwittingly walking into deadly danger, under-equipped and unprepared.

Which was exactly what they were supposed to think. Yonker and Xai had reasoned that such a low-key incursion would not require immediate action from whoever might be guarding Gerhard's base – mercs or poachers or rangers, or a mix of the three. Let the unsuspecting 'primitives' blunder into danger; they could easily be taken out . . .

'Get ready, eh?' hissed Yonker. Senosi spoke to his warriors in his own tongue – whether giving instructions or a last-minute pep talk, Grant didn't know.

Grant checked for the hundredth time that he was holding Moth's catty correctly and his ammo was good to go. Senosi's people had shown Moth how to drill into tree bark to get sticky sap – and how to use it to upgrade stones into weapons that could take out a titanoboa. She'd carefully filed the sides of the stones to sharp edges and rubbed them in beetle larvae poison. Grant had a whole bunch of them in his pouch and had wrapped strips of fabric around his fingertips to protect him from accidental scratches.

'Not safe!' Roland bellowed at Moth and Xai as they drew closer. 'It's a trap! Get back!'

Xai and Moth didn't heed Roland's warning, but Xai's hand crept towards the shank of fabric over his shoulder.

Suddenly, as if the intruders had crossed some invisible line, there was movement from a ramshackle outbuilding perhaps twenty metres behind Roland. An enormous serpent uncoiled, pushing itself across the dusty land towards the intruders at horrible speed. Its jaws were wide open, gruesome fangs curving out, as long as ice picks.

But Xai stood his ground. He grabbed a grenade from the strap beneath the fabric, pulled the pin and lobbed it – straight down the snake's gullet. At the same time, Moth hurled her spear, which caught in the titanoboa's scaly body. The snake hissed and shuddered. Xai and Moth turned and raced away. But Grant knew with sickening certainty that the snake would be faster. It chased after them and reared up, ready to bring down its terrifying jaws –

Until it blew apart in a gory explosion as the grenade detonated.

'Take out the CCTV camera,' Roland called hoarsely, jerking his head towards the building behind him. Xai produced a gun and shot it twice. The second bullet blew the camera apart.

At the same time, Yonker lobbed a grenade at the fence, close to a CCTV camera mounted on a supporting pole. Grant lowered his head and covered his ears as the grenade exploded. Dust and dirt showered down all around, and when he looked again, the wire fence was torn and twisted open, a dusty crater blown open at its base.

But as the haze began to clear, Grant saw another giant titanoboa already sidewinding towards them.

Ralph was trying to breathe through his shirt. His throat was stinging and he felt light-headed. He'd heard explosions outside, was terrified about what might have happened. But when the loud metallic rattle of a key turning on the other side of the door sounded, he willed himself to focus. He nodded to Luke, who nodded back, wide-eyed and frightened.

Then the heavy door handle swung upwards and the thick cold-room door opened. A man, wearing a face mask and carrying a handgun, peered cautiously into the room. Luke grabbed him with both hands and dragged him forward, propelling him into the smoke. Another man came in, also wielding a revolver. Ralph threw a punch, but knew he was too slow and sluggish from the smoke: the man feinted out of the way. But Luke was faster, and brought both fists down on the back of the man's neck. As the guard fell to his knees, Ralph tried to grab the gun, but the man would not relinquish it.

'Come on!' Luke yelled. 'Before reinforcements arrive!'

Cursing, Ralph abandoned his struggle for the gun and dived out of the room. Luke slammed the door shut and locked it.

Ralph lay on the floor, panting. 'What if they suffocate in there?'

Over the whine of the alarm there were two gunshots and the sound of breaking glass.

'They've got ventilation now. And they can stuff the sheet in the incinerator and slam the door to stop it smoking.' Luke dragged Ralph to his feet. 'How about we try worrying about ourselves –'

'And find that data centre,' Ralph agreed, starting off along the corridor as muffled shouts and crashes sounded from behind the door. 'If those snakes can't be stopped, there's gonna be a bloodbath!'

For Grant, the sight of the titanoboa so close brought a terror so primal, it was all he could do not to turn and run gibbering into the bush. But Yonker stood up and sprayed the monster with rounds from the AK-47. The bullets beat into the beast's hide, but they were unable to pierce it. As Yonker kept going, Grant fired off the catapult as fast as he could. But his first two rocks bounced off the beast, and only three spears out of the eight thrown by the tribespeople managed to penetrate their target.

And then the titanoboa smashed through the ruins of the fence and was suddenly there in front of them, a quivering mass of rage and bile, hissing and spitting, red eyes like blazing coals in its face. Yonker fell to one knee and fired up at its mouth, chipping ivory from its fangs. The snake lunged for him, its mouth closing around his head and shoulders, but Yonker jammed the rifle lengthways into those terrible jaws so they couldn't close. Hissing wildly, the snake smashed into Senosi, knocking him flat. A Bakho man tried to grip the rippling body, stabbing at it with Yonker's commando knife, but the snake shook him free then used its head as a battering ram to smash two more men to the ground. Grant lost his footing and fell on his back, which caused the snake to notice him for the first time. It hissed harder, acidic saliva dripping from its wedged-open jaws.

As the great head came down to crush his chest, Grant raised the catty and fired. One of Moth's poisoned missiles struck its left eye, which burst open with a disgusting wet plop. The snake started to thrash around in agony, blood spurting from the ruined socket. The surviving Bakho warriors hurled themselves at the predasaur along its hideous length, working together, gripping hold of it and trying to pin it down. Yonker pulled a revolver from a hip holster. Grant closed his eyes, and heard the gunshot. Then there was silence.

Grant shuddered. He helped Senosi up from the ground. Tears streaked his face.

'Gope is dead,' he said, pointing to one of his fallen comrades. 'It cannot be for nothing. We've done so much to fight in secret. Now it is time to fight back in the open.'

'And we'd better get going,' said Grant, looking to where Xai and Moth were working to free Roland from his chains. 'Looks like they could use some help. We'll have lost the element of surprise now.'

'And we don't know how many more of those oversized jelly snakes they've got in store for us,' Yonker said, pushing his way through the splintered fence.

'Only one way to find out,' Grant muttered, and followed Yonker into the compound.

The alarms had shut off. Robyn felt the world growing more distant around her. She felt light-headed, her arms and legs filled with pins and needles. Her skin was soaked with sweat and her head throbbed. She could hear, behind her, Abi cleaning and sterilising a syringe for the medic, cooling the barrel with ether spray to lower the chance of clotting. Robyn looked at the cannula protruding from her wrist, secured in place with a bulldog clip to avoid further damage to the vein, and wondered how much blood she'd already given, and how much more she had to lose.

She heard raised voices from the room next door, though they might as well have come from a thousand miles away.

'CCTV's down,' Gerhard shouted. 'I need eyes out there.'

A woman's voice came, anxious and puzzled: 'Life signs

of second titanoboa registered a huge spike in adrenaline, then nothing.'

'They can't both be dead!' Gerhard was seething. 'How can two primitive tribespeople kill a –'

'It's got to be Ballantyne's friends, disguised,' Abrafo raged. 'I said you were a fool to leave Ballantyne above ground.'

'You want to get paid?' Gerhard snarled. 'Get Ballantyne! Stop whatever's going on.' A pause. Then: 'You – go with them.' (Who was he talking to now? Robyn wasn't sure.) 'Take *that* with you. Do whatever it takes to make the thing responsive. I take it *those* vital signs are still online, at least?'

The words didn't make sense any more. It didn't matter. 'Dad,' Robyn breathed, struggling to sit up from the trolley she lay on. 'Got to help Dad . . .'

Abi turned from Niko with a bloodied syringe and pushed Robyn firmly back down. 'From the sound of things,' she said, 'it's whoever set off that alarm that's going to need all the help they can get.'

Grant was first to catch up with Moth and Xai; they'd reached Roland and were hammering with rocks at the point where the chains that bound his ankle met the post. They were flattening the heavy link but couldn't break it.

Roland beamed at Grant as he came near. 'Good to see you.'

'Mutual,' Grant said, and passed Xai a piece of twisted gate post blown off by the grenade. 'Here. Might work as a crowbar?'

'It might,' Xai said, and set to work.

'There was an alarm inside the facility,' Roland said. 'It's stopped.'

Grant jumped at the sound of two muffled gunshots and glass breaking. He saw thick smoke blowing out from the window of a bunker perhaps fifty metres away. 'What's going on?'

'Nothing we can't make worse!' Yonker had arrived. He helped Xai to lever the improvised crowbar against the heavy chain link. It gave, just as the Bakho warriors arrived with Senosi.

Moth snatched the catty from Grant's pocket. 'Thanks for looking after this.'

'It saved our lives, Motholeli,' Senosi told her. 'And it reminds me – the smallest of weapons can bring down the biggest of enemies.'

Grant smiled. 'When we first met, you said no one ever noticed you. Guess you were wrong.'

Moth looked down shyly, but Grant saw pride in her face.

Roland picked up the length of chain attached to his ankle. 'No time to take this off now,' he said. 'Whatever else is happening in there, Robyn and Ralph and Niko are inside. And Gerhard, Abrafo, Rontane . . .'

'Quite the party, eh?' Yonker said, loading a fresh clip into his AK-47. 'Time we crashed it.'

'That's the way in.' Roland pointed to an unassuming, dilapidated old building. 'There's a hidden lift inside –'

His words were cut off as the doors to the building were kicked open and two poachers appeared with rifles. Before anyone could react, Moth had loosed a stone from her catty. It struck the poacher on the left straight in the forehead. As he twisted with the impact, his rifle barrel caught his comrade under the chin, knocking him backwards.

Yonker laughed and slapped a hand on Moth's shoulder as she breathed out shakily. 'Now you're just showing off!'

The Bakho warriors were not wasting the advantage Moth had won. They ran straight for the doors. One of them produced a blowpipe from his quiver and fired something at the fallen men, who twitched and then lay still. Another confiscated the poachers' weapons and held them aloft to show Senosi, who called to him approvingly in Bakho.

Xai looked at Senosi. 'They sleep?'

'Yes.' Senosi smiled thinly. 'But not for ever.'

'Let's hope we catch the rest napping,' said Roland, as Yonker passed him a handgun. 'We have to get my children and Niko to safety.'

'And take back what is ours,' Senosi added.

'And cleanse the land of Gerhard's homemade monsters,' said Yonker.

Amen to all that, thought Grant, as Roland led the advance, braced for the final battle.

29

Since the fire alarm had cut out, Ralph's ears were ringing. He wanted to tear through the corridors, but Luke's limp was holding them back big-time.

Ralph felt sick to think about what injuries Luke must have sustained when the cave hyenas had attacked, but he was also well aware of the CCTV cameras positioned throughout the building. He wondered who else would come to investigate the fire in the mortuary, and how long it would be before the staff trapped inside were freed. Then again, they hadn't come across anyone evacuating yet, so the compound could only be running with a skeleton staff.

Perhaps we stand a chance, Ralph thought. *If we can find the server room, knock out the titanoboas so it's safe to get to Dad . . .*

They passed a door in the wall. Ralph opened it, but it was only a storeroom, filled with huge drums of purified water.

'Where d'you think the servers will be?' he asked Luke.

'No clue without knowing the layout,' Luke said, grimacing as he tried to match Ralph's pace along the corridor. 'I mean . . . the data centre might be off-site for all we know.'

'Off-site?' Ralph groaned. 'How are we meant to get to it, then? We saw those snakes take up position. If we go out above ground, they'll kill us –'

'So, we search down here first,' Luke said.

But as they rounded the corner Ralph froze. At the end of the corridor was Rontane. She stood with one of the men who'd escorted Ralph here with the titanoboas; now, as then, he was holding a tablet.

Rontane spotted the boys. 'Get them!' she screamed.

But Ralph was already turning, pushing Luke ahead of him.

'I can't outrun them,' Luke hissed.

'I know. Hide in that storeroom,' said Ralph. 'I'll try to lead them away. When it's clear, start looking for the data centre again.'

'I will.' Luke slipped into the storeroom and Ralph closed the door quietly before running ahead. He lingered near a junction, waiting for Rontane and her ally to come into sight so he could be sure they would follow him.

But it wasn't Rontane he saw, or the man with the tablet. Instead, the dark hulk of a rhino covered in coarse hair appeared. He'd seen it on Gerhard's tour – it was clearly a juvenile, but its head was already at his chest height. Its eyes were pink, and the horn curving up from its bestial forehead looked tough enough to bore through Ralph's ribcage.

Wrong-footed, Ralph tried to think. The rhino must have

escaped from somewhere. Then he pictured the man with the tablet, and guessed that it wasn't only snakes Gerhard was working to control; even now, his assistant was seeing out of the dim eyes of a beast constructed from an unholy mixture of ancient DNA and cutting-edge science.

'I guess it does work for four legs as well as none,' Ralph breathed. 'Damn it.'

The creature took a few faltering steps towards him. Ralph knew that modern-day rhinos didn't have great vision, so their instinct was to charge at the unknown in case it was a threat that could be scared away. But this Ice Age throwback's instincts would have been supplanted by the murderous desire of its creator, and Ralph knew that any charge could only end with deadly force.

He turned and ran as the woolly rhino broke into a stumbling charge. Behind him he could hear the uncertain stomp of its heavy feet, like a giant drumming its fingers. Ralph knew it could outrun him; his only chance lay in making it change direction to slow it down.

Skidding around a sharp corner, Ralph pushed himself faster. There was an almighty crash behind him that almost knocked him off his feet; unable to change course in time, the rhino had shoulder-charged the wall. Its feet slipping on the smooth floor tiles, the rhino started running again.

Panic-stricken, Ralph barged through a fire door and found himself at the top of a dimly lit staircase. Surely steps would slow down a rhinoceros? Ralph hurled himself down the steps three at a time. The beast behind him smashed through the door and didn't hesitate – it stumbled on, banging against the concrete walls and slipping on the steps, its gasps and grunts of pain and anger growing hoarser, louder in Ralph's ears.

One single thought hammered through his mind, as relentless as the rhino's footfalls. *It's gaining on me.*

Finally, Ralph ran out of staircase and into a concrete cul-de-sac, bare but for a dark green wooden door. He tried it.

Locked.

The woolly rhino, frantic and bloodied from its descent of the staircase, thundered down the last steps towards Ralph, out of control.

Grant stood in the ruins of the miners' canteen, staring out of the door. He and Moth were standing guard while Roland, Xai, Yonker and the Bakho searched methodically for a way to access the lower levels. The button that Roland had seen Gerhard press to summon the hidden lift no longer seemed to work.

Moth pointed to what looked like a dust storm gathering in the distance. There was a dark, roiling whirlwind inside the thick cloud. 'Hey, everyone – titanoboa coming this way. Close the door.'

'That thing wouldn't keep out a hungry aardvark,' said Yonker, hurrying over to the doorway. Roland and Xai joined him, firearms cocked and ready, and Yonker took another grenade from his shoulder strap, pulled the pin and hurled it overarm into the path of the giant snake. But to Grant's horror, the titanoboa simply turned sharply away from its original course, neatly skirting the grenade as it fragmented in a blistering blast.

'It's being controlled, like the others,' Grant said. 'They must be able to see what it sees.'

'Then let them see bullets!' Xai hissed, and he and Roland opened fire on the writhing monstrosity. It retreated, waiting until they had exhausted their ammo, then surged back towards them. Moth fired stone after stone, but only one embedded itself in the deadly serpent, not enough to finish it.

Senosi spoke quietly to his warriors in Bakho, and they trooped outside to fight. 'We'll keep the snake occupied out there,' Senosi told Roland. 'The time we buy you . . .'

'We'll use it.' Roland grasped his hand in a firm shake. 'Use it well.'

The titanoboa was hissing as it wound closer with horrible speed. Boldly, Senosi stepped outside to face it with the warriors.

'I'm going to help them,' Xai said. Roland and Yonker began to argue, but he shouted over them. 'Grant – close the door after me.'

Grant hesitated. And in that split-second, Moth slipped out after Xai.

'No!' Yonker started after her even as the door slammed shut. Then a gunshot rang out. Yonker gasped, went rigid, then collapsed.

'What?' Grant stared at Yonker's fallen body in horror. Roland, with a soldier's professional training, had turned and raised his weapon immediately.

Only to find he could not fire.

Abrafo stepped out of the hidden lift. Grant stared in disbelief: the poacher was holding Luke in a neck-lock, and had a revolver jammed up against his temple.

'Found this joke of a boy hiding in a storeroom,' he snarled. 'Drop your weapon, Ballantyne, before I drop the kid's brains all over the floor.'

Luke closed his eyes, shaking with fear. 'Please don't kill me.'

Roland looked at Yonker, then at Grant. Then he closed his eyes and dropped the gun. Outside, Senosi's warriors yelled battle cries and bullets fired.

'Let's move,' Abrafo said. 'Get in this lift, now. Hands on your heads. Don't try anything, or this punk pays the price.'

Grant placed his hands on the back of his head, as Roland did the same.

'Where are my children?' Roland demanded.

'Your daughter's dying on the operating table.' Abrafo smirked as they entered the lift. 'As for your son –'

'There was a rhino,' Luke said, his voice a hoarse rasp through Abrafo's chokehold. 'Woolly rhino . . .'

'Chased him right down to the lowest level, by the sounds of it,' Abrafo agreed brightly. 'Still, Rontane ought to have scraped what's left of him off the floor by now. Press the button for floor –3, Khumalo, and we'll check it out.'

Grant hit the –3 button and the door slid closed.

'Going down,' Abrafo murmured, dark eyes shining.

For Ralph, as the woolly rhinoceros closed the distance between them, time seemed to slow. At the last possible moment, Ralph flung himself aside and the beast charged into the door, knocking it down with a splintering crash that left the rhino screeching with pain and anger. Its legs gave way and it fell, its momentum sending it skidding into the shadows.

A foul stink wafted from out of the dark. Feeling sick from the rush of adrenaline, Ralph started to force himself back up the stairs. But he could hear footsteps coming down towards him, and familiar voices.

'We need the boy,' Rontane announced to her companion, 'or what's left of him. Show his head to Ballantyne and he'll know we're not bluffing when it comes to killing his girl . . .'

Fear clawed at Ralph's chest, but he wasn't giving up now. He turned and crept through the splintered door into the warm, fetid darkness. A heavy thrum of power was coming from somewhere ahead. *Generators*, Ralph realised. Like Crocodile Lodge – which was far enough away from urban infrastructure to need its own microgrid – this place must tick over on a battery energy storage system fed by the solar panels, with diesel generators kicking in when necessary. Perhaps if he could take out the power down here, the predasaur beasts would be free, and Gerhard wouldn't be able to control them?

His feet splashed softly; either a pipe had burst, or floodwater must have drained into this basement area without Gerhard knowing. Suddenly he realised he couldn't hear the woolly rhino. Was the beast unconscious? No sounds of movement carried over the penetrating high-voltage hum. But the thick, musky smell was getting stronger.

Gingerly, Ralph felt his way through the pitch blackness and came up hard against something metal. First, he thought it was a cage; then he realised he was flanked by wide, flat prongs. Reaching forward into the 'cage', he felt a steering wheel. *It's a forklift truck*, he realised. Turning aside and groping blindly, he came up against some wooden shelving units; they would offer some cover, at least.

'Ralph?' Rontane's voice carried through the dark; she had moved softly and sounded horribly close. 'No good hiding, boy. It's all gone too far. Time we ended things.'

Ralph moved as quietly as he dared over the damp ground, retreating behind the shelving.

He heard the click of a safety catch. 'I'll end it quickly, Ralph,' Rontane said. 'Man, where's that damn light switch?'

'Here somewhere,' the technician muttered from nearer the doorway.

Finally there was a *thunk* of a heavy switch being thrown, and a fiery orange light warmed the room from a large bulb hanging down from the ceiling. Ralph blinked furiously to clear his eyes. He saw the banks of batteries stacked parallel to the basement wall, each trailing a thick spaghetti of cables up along the brickwork to the ceiling. Rontane held a hunting rifle, pointing it at the shadows as she turned in a slow, deliberate circle.

But, squinting into the gloom at head height, Rontane failed to notice a movement at her feet. Something stirring in the black floodwater.

Ralph felt paralysed with horror. It was as if the dark tentacles of some monstrous creature were breaking the scummy surface. But then his eyes made sense of what he was seeing, and he held his breath once more.

Each sinuous strand of scaly flesh was alive.

Each was a boa constrictor with raw, bloodshot eyes. These creatures were a normal size, not huge and thick like the titanoboas he'd seen earlier, and their skin looked smoother, almost transparent.

Ralph realised that the snakes were very young. Babies.

And that the colossal titanoboa slowly emerging from its lair behind the batteries must be their mother.

30

The technician screamed out a frantic warning. Ralph jumped. Rontane spun around, saw the serpent dart from out of the shadows, and opened fire. But the young snakes attacked the poacher together, slithering up her legs and coiling around her torso. Rontane cried out, dropped the gun and tried to prise the snakes away, but they climbed up her body and tightened their grip. She doubled over. Ralph saw her eyes fix on his own in awful, pleading silence. Her face contorted with agony, but not a sound shook out from her. The snakes' tails wound around her neck like living ropes, garrotting her, cutting tighter and tighter. Her eyes bulged and her face turned crimson, until finally her lifeless body fell, stiff as a tree trunk, the snakes still clinging to it like ivy.

The trundling slide of a lift door opening broke the shocked silence, then the babble of the technician as he ran for it. 'Let me in! We can't control those monsters –'

'Shut up!' Abrafo snarled as he stepped out of the lift. Ralph's heart felt like it might swallow itself.

'The titanoboas can breed!' the technician cried. 'The experiment's out of control, we have to –'

'I said, *shut up*!' Abrafo's words were punctuated by a pistol shot. The technician staggered backwards, a crimson stain swelling over his white coat, disbelief on his face.

Then the jaws of the mother titanoboa closed around him.

Finally, Ralph screamed.

'There.' Robyn heard Abi's voice as if it came from the other side of the moon. 'We've done all we can.'

Robyn's eyes flickered open. She felt heavy and sick. There was Niko, lying on the trolley, barely visible beneath an oxygen mask, electrodes, tubes and wires. A portable diagnostic unit beeped steadily next to her.

'When . . . will you know?' Robyn murmured.

'You've pulled through, Robyn. You're stronger than you look,' said the medic. 'The next eight hours will be crucial. Abi, stay with them. I'll tell Gerhard the procedure's finished.'

After he left, Abi looked down at Robyn. 'Well, now. Here we are. Alone together. No one watching.'

Robyn felt a shiver of fear as Abi took a step closer, her blue eyes icy hard.

'Yes,' Abi breathed. 'It's really finished.'

She raised a syringe and loomed over Robyn.

Just like Roland, Luke and Abrafo, Grant stared in horror as the thrashing technician was swallowed by the giant serpent. And as Ralph's cry carried over the glottal sucking noises, Roland looked shaken to his core.

'Ralph?' he bellowed.

Grant seized his chance. Abrafo hadn't moved his gun back to threaten Luke since shooting the technician – perhaps in shock at the scene playing out in front of him. Now Grant flattened his hand and chopped it down on Abrafo's wrist. The poacher dropped the gun, which clattered to the floor beside the stagnant water – and at the same moment, Luke threw himself forward, tearing free of Abrafo's grip and sending the poacher off balance.

Roland seized his chance with both hands. With a roar he dragged the poacher out of the lift and into the fetid basement. But Abrafo twisted and broke Roland's grip. Landing on his knees, he pushed forward and butted Roland in the stomach. Roland fell back into the shallow water.

Grant saw a snake as thick as a man's leg rise from Rontane's body and rear up over Roland. Snatching the fallen gun, Grant fired and the snake fell back. At the same time, Roland punched Abrafo in the neck, put a foot to his chest and pushed him back. Luke grabbed hold of the poacher and got him in a neck-lock. But Abrafo bit down on Luke's arm and elbowed him in the ribs. Luke fell back, banging his head on the ground, and lay still as Abrafo bellowed his defiance, his teeth stained red with Luke's blood.

Grant went to fire a warning shot over Abrafo's head. But the chamber was empty; the gun was useless. He saw that the mother titanoboa had finished with the technician and now its hellish red eyes were sweeping about, looking for its next prey.

'Help me, someone!' Ralph shouted.

Roland tried to go to him, but Abrafo grabbed hold of him again.

It's down to me, thought Grant.

As Roland and Abrafo grappled, Grant ran through the water and jumped the hissing frenzy of the snakes. For a second he couldn't see Ralph. Then he saw movement in the forklift truck – Ralph was leaning in, grappling with something. It was Rontane's gun.

'I'm trying to jam it in place,' he said. 'Help me.'

Grant understood. 'Jam it against the accelerator pedal?'

Ralph nodded quickly. 'We have one of these at the lodge for shifting cages. If we can get the angle right . . .'

'We can put it in gear and spear that thing!' Grant agreed.

Even as he spoke, the titanoboa surged forward. A curved fang caught the side of the forklift and nearly knocked it over. Ralph fell backwards, sprawling on the floor.

The titanoboa gave a hiss of triumph as it zeroed in on its target, its jaws open wide. Grant grabbed at Ralph's arm and pulled him clear just in the nick of time. Then he caught a blur of movement from the shadows: a dark, shaggy form breaking from the back of the basement to charge.

It was a woolly rhino, its hide bloody, its horn broken. But anger was giving it strength. The titanoboa's head swung down and it looked at the rhino. The rhino charged it, and a shockwave rippled through the snake's bloated scaly body, like a giant shaking out a lasso. The snake slammed into the battery store and lay there, stunned. In seconds, two smaller boas were wrapping themselves around the woolly rhino, which stomped angrily in a circle, trying to shake its attackers off. It bundled into Roland and Abrafo, who were still fighting. Abrafo screamed as a heavy foot stamped on his ankle, and he fell back in the water. Roland jumped onto the juvenile beast's back like he'd joined a rodeo, desperately gripping the fur on its neck.

'Don't just sit there watching!' Ralph was back wrestling with the forklift's controls, sticking it into gear. 'Hit the power!'

Grant reached forward into the truck and slammed his fingers against a green button. There was a loud electric whine and an orange light flashed on the roof of the forklift. Then the vehicle raced towards the titanoboa.

But it was too slow. The snake easily moved out of the way. Grant could've screamed with frustration.

But he hadn't banked on what happened next. The twin spears missed the huge body but penetrated the racks of batteries. High-voltage charge spat from inside with a fierce crackle, conducted by the floodwater. The overhead light flashed like a strobe, showing the titanoboa squealing and convulsing in ghastly snatches of motion as the electricity overwhelmed it. Abrafo, too, jerked and rocked in the flow of power, screaming in agony, until the thrashing serpent fell, a dead weight . . .

. . . and its fangs speared the poacher through the chest. He gave a last, gurgling groan of agony.

Mercifully, the light bulb shattered and all light was extinguished.

'Is everyone all right?' Ralph yelled.

Grant put a hand on Ralph's shoulder. Held his breath. Waited for the longest time in silence.

Then pale grey emergency lights clunked on in the ceiling. Roland Ballantyne stood in front of them, supporting Luke beside him. They were bruised and bloody but smiling. Roland hugged his son.

'We're all right,' Roland said. 'Got out of the water just before the batteries went in.'

Ralph just held him in silence. Grant found himself wishing that he could hold his own father in the same way.

'Even that damn woolly rhino's all right,' Luke said, shaking his head in disbelief. He laughed, relief shining through his weariness.

Roland extricated himself from Ralph's grip and went to check on the titanoboa. 'Dead,' he reported. 'And thank God. In extreme cases female boas can produce live young without mating – it's called parthenogenesis. But for spontaneous birth to have occurred in a Frankenstein species like the *predasaur* . . .'

'They really can't be controlled,' Ralph muttered. 'Whatever Gerhard thinks.'

Roland had moved on to Abrafo's body. It was bloodied and horribly burnt.

Ralph grimaced. 'That's the end of him, right?'

'Finally.' Roland showed no triumph; his voice was empty of emotion. 'Perhaps if I'd finished things better all those years ago, things would be different now. Perhaps Yonker would be –'

'Back to annoy your sorry asses!' a familiar voice boomed from the gloom.

'Yonker!' Roland crossed to embrace him. 'You're all right?'

'After the last time I got shot, you think I wouldn't wear a combat vest under my clothes?' He slapped Roland on the back. 'Now, my old chommie, don't waste the love on me. After taking down that damn snake outside, we could *all* use some sweetness . . .'

Grant looked past Yonker and saw Moth limp into sight from the stairway, helping Xai, and Senosi, supported by one of his warriors.

'The others?' Grant asked softly. 'Did they make it?'

Moth looked at Senosi, then shook her head sadly.

'Come on,' Roland said. 'We still have to find Robyn and Niko.'

'And Gerhard,' said Ralph. 'Let's finish this.'

'Abi!' Gerhard was banging on the glass observation window. 'Get the Ballantyne girl out here.'

'She's sleeping, sir,' Abi reported.

'Then wheel her out. Now!' The medic was trying to show Gerhard something on the tablet, but Gerhard just shoved him away. 'The titanoboas are dead. I can't raise my rangers on the radio, not even those damned poachers . . .' Abruptly, the lights died. A pale luminescence seeped from emergency bulbs high in the wall.

'The power's out.' Abi studied Niko's vital signs monitor, which had switched automatically to the emergency power supply. 'Ballantyne's mob must be on their way.'

'Of course they are,' Gerhard snapped, putting on a face mask. 'And there's no one left to stop them. So, bring Robyn out here. At least then we'll have something to bargain with.'

Abi looked down at Robyn, lying so still beneath the crisp white sheet. Slowly, she pushed the trolley out of the operating room to join Gerhard in the adjacent area.

'There she is,' Gerhard said, looking down at Robyn. 'The girl who'll make me the richest man on Earth and ensure I live to collect . . .' He peered more closely at her then turned to Abi and frowned. 'She's not dead? She can't be.' Panic-stricken, he bent over to put his ear to her chest. 'I need her to keep Ballantyne at bay. I need her blood, she can't be –'

'*Dead*?' Robyn pulled her right hand from under the sheet – in it, she clutched the syringe that Abi had given her – and plunged the hypodermic needle deep into Gerhard's neck. He gasped, jerked away, and pulled out the needle. A little jet of blood arced out. He stared at the syringe in his hand, looking shaken and affronted.

'What the hell!' he spluttered. 'Abigail?'

'Sorry, sir,' Abi said calmly. 'I'm afraid you've just been injected with curare. We use it on the predasaurs to treat the muscle spasms you've induced in them.'

'There was enough there to put out a cave hyena,' Robyn added, swinging herself into a sitting position. 'So, more than enough to end you.'

'You'll never get out of here,' Gerhard hissed coldly. 'Mbato is sending an extraction squad –'

'So, ring him now and warn him to call it off, before the curare does its thing,' said Abi. 'You have about four minutes before full body paralysis sets in. You'll be unconscious in five minutes, dead in under ten.'

'Unless we give you this antidote,' said Robyn, revealing another syringe in her left hand. She passed it to Abi. 'Call Mbato now. Tell him someone got careless with the virus samples. This place has to stay in quarantine for seventy-two hours.'

'Pathetic.' Gerhard staggered and leaned heavily against the wall. 'You think . . . think I'm going to . . .'

'Going to do anything we ask?' said Robyn. 'Yes, we do. And right now.'

'Because you really don't have long,' Abi said. 'And you'd better sell it to Mbato good, so he stays away.' She sneered at him. 'Do it. Or die.'

Gerhard licked his dry lips. 'If I do, you'll let me die anyway.'

'Why would we do that to you . . . when we can do *this*?' Abi held up her phone and played a voice memo. '*I'll transfer funds to the usual account, Abrafo,*' Mbato's voice said. '*With deductions in place for failing to hand over Xai and the Khumalo boy.*'

'*You got the Ballantynes!*' Abrafo protested. '*They're the real targets.*'

'*Strictly speaking,*' Gerhard said smoothly, '*it was me who successfully abducted the Ballantyne children.*'

'Oh yes,' said Robyn as Abi paused the message. 'See, we really do want you alive, Gerhard. You can clear our names *and* confess to what you've done. And you will.'

With a look of pure hatred, Gerhard took out his phone and called Mbato. It went to voicemail, and he left a message. Abi waited tensely. She doubted that Gerhard had ever taken an order in his life – but she also doubted that he had ever stared death quite so openly in the face either.

He kept the details to a minimum. His voice was beginning to slur. 'I'll hope to hear from you soon, Julius.' His grey eyes were fixed viciously on Robyn and Abi as he spoke. 'And don't fret. You'll get your hands on our prisoners soon enough.'

He hung up, just as the door banged open. Abi retreated behind Robyn as a dishevelled, ragtag group charged inside: Roland, Ralph, the van Rok boy. Xai and Senosi. A big bear of a man, and a girl with a catty . . .

'Dad!' Robyn cried, clinging to him as he wrapped her in his arms. 'Ralph!' Ralph piled in and hugged them both.

The big man seized Abi with less affection.

'Don't,' Robyn said. 'She's with us. After what's happened, she hates Gerhard as much as we do.'

'Give me the antidote,' Gerhard rasped. 'Give it to me!'

Xai pointed a gun at Gerhard. 'Don't move.'

'He won't be able to,' said Abi, 'if I don't give him this adrenaline shot.'

Gerhard sank to the floor, twitching. 'Save me,' he groaned as his eyes flickered shut. 'Save . . . me . . .'

'How about that,' Abi murmured. 'The big bad genius actually believed I'd give him enough curare to kill him.'

'He'll be asleep for a good long time,' said Robyn.

'Then . . . it's over.' Senosi was crouching over the bags of plant matter Rontane had dumped on the floor. 'The virus cure – there's still a chance we can develop it. Help the world.'

'A good chance,' Abi agreed, 'judging by Niko's vital signs. In a few hours we'll know more but it's looking good.'

'We're not exactly out of the woods yet, but I think we're all going to be all right.' Robyn smiled. 'And guys, come on. What took you so long?'

EPILOGUE

Twenty-four hours later, Ralph had showered, changed and rested. The staff had quarters on site – enough rooms for everyone to have one to themselves. After so long sleeping in a car, or in a tree, or not sleeping at all, the feel of a soft bunk had felt completely alien. To get any sleep at all, Ralph had had to lie on the floor.

He'd feared bad dreams, but sleep had passed in a gritty-eyed blur and he felt better for it, as he told his sister when he found her – not in her room, of course, but in the recovery pen with the juvenile woolly rhino. Abi had patched up the beast, and he was resting, like they all were.

'I'm beginning to feel halfway human,' Ralph remarked.

'Halfway? For you, that must be a record,' said Robyn with a smile. She was looking into the animal's pink eyes. It made Ralph feel uneasy: a prehistoric beast, bred just a matter of months ago.

'That thing saved a lot of lives in the power room,' Ralph said quietly, trying to feel more grateful.

'He has a spirit,' Robyn said firmly. 'A soul. Despite

everything Gerhard did to him. I can reach him, help him. I know I can.'

Ralph thought of Gerhard, tied up in an office chair with Xai standing guard over him. *See how he likes being the prisoner*, thought Ralph vengefully. But he felt uneasy. Dad had said they needed to leave by tomorrow to avoid the extraction squad Mbato would inevitably send. By then, Niko should be recovered enough to move out with them safely. They would take Gerhard with them too – find a way to make him clear their name. Luke's computer skills had got them inside the data server (which they'd discovered was beside the projected 'film set' Ralph had witnessed), and he'd hacked his way through security so that Roland and Grant could peruse evidence on all angles of Gerhard's sick researches.

But somehow, Ralph couldn't imagine Gerhard taking defeat lying down. And they still had to make it out of the mountains and back to civilisation if they were to expose Mbato and convince the world that it was Gerhard who had created the new pandemic, not their family. Ralph wondered if he would ever feel safe again.

'I'll be glad if you can reach the rhino,' said Ralph. 'I'm just relieved you're here at all, to be honest. I mean, I thought you were . . . well. You know.'

'Yeah, I know.' Robyn looked at him. 'You too. Thought you must be dead for sure.'

'And yet, somehow, we're not.' Ralph smiled wryly. 'Maybe we should call it the Luke effect.'

'I still can't believe he made it.' Robyn's smile faded. 'Or that we did. We've been so lucky. Luckier than Senosi's people, anyway.'

Ralph swallowed hard, remembering the emotions that had washed over him when they'd buried the Bakho warriors in the dusty land outside the compound: land that truly belonged to them, whatever the government might say.

'I guess Grant's little friend Moth is lucky, at least,' said Ralph. 'Senosi says she can hang with the tribe if she wants, learn more about her heritage. Course, he'll be busy trying to perfect his virus miracle cure for a while . . . but when they're ready to share with the authorities, he wants her to come on the road with him, talk about the issues affecting her people.'

'And will she?'

'Grant's not sure.'

'It's not realistic for Senosi to work by himself,' said Robyn firmly. 'Too many people need that cure, like, yesterday. I think Niko's suggestion that he work with her colleagues at Sangomed is a good one.'

Ralph smiled. 'It's still so weird you're, like, besties with Niko now.'

'Well, I have to like her, don't I?' Robyn said. 'She's got my blood in her.'

'Makes her a Ballantyne,' Ralph said. 'Family.'

The door opened, and Grant peered inside. 'Hey, Robyn!' he began enthusiastically, then he saw Ralph sitting beside her and couldn't quite hide a look of disappointment. 'Uh . . . hi, Ralph. You OK?'

'Getting there.'

'Great. Me too.' Grant cleared his throat. 'Just came to say, Yonker's ready to leave with Abi.'

'Right, of course,' Ralph said. Yonker was letting Moth stay with the tribe while he drove Abi across the border. 'Off she goes to start a quiet new life, lying low in Mozambique.'

'Shows that some people can change,' Robyn said.

'If they meet the right people,' Ralph agreed. 'And God knows, we need to meet the right people if we're gonna stand a chance of making it back to our old lives.'

'Or start new ones,' Grant murmured, looking at Robyn. Then he shrugged self-consciously. 'Anyway! He's going, and Moth's off to stay with the Bakho while they're gone, and . . . stuff. See ya down there.'

Grant exited. Ralph gave Robyn a look. 'I was gonna say we're all kind of like family now. But I'm thinking you want Grant to stay more of a friend . . . or something.'

'Or something,' Robyn said with a faint smile. 'But before any of us can start something new, we have to end this.'

'Then let's wave off Abi and Yonker and Moth and Senosi, and get back to saving our strength.' Ralph looked at his sister. 'Something tells me we're going to need it.'

DISCOVER HOW THE PREDASAURS WERE FIRST UNLEASHED . . .

Out now.

Wilbur Smith is one of the most successful authors in the world, having sold over 130 million copies of his incredible adventure novels. Wilbur died in 2021, leaving behind him a treasure-trove of stories that will delight readers for years to come.

Keith Chapman is a television writer and producer, best known as the creator of children's television programmes *Bob the Builder* and *PAW Patrol*. Keith originates from Norfolk and currently resides in Monaco.

Steve Cole is the best-selling author of over 150 books. His work includes the *Astrosaurs* series, original fiction titles for *Doctor Who*, the *Young Bond* series and *Swarm Rising* co-authored with astronaut Tim Peake. Steve lives and works in Buckinghamshire.

For all the latest information about Wilbur, visit:
www.wilbursmithbooks.com
facebook.com/WilburSmith
www.wilbur-niso-smithfoundation.org

THE WILBUR &
NISO SMITH
FOUNDATION

Thank you for choosing a Hot Key book.

For all the latest bookish news, freebies and exclusive
content, sign up to the Hot Key newsletter – scan the

QR code or visit lnk.to/HotKeyBooks

Follow us on social media:

bonnierbooks.co.uk/HotKeyBooks